WHEN I'M WITH YOU

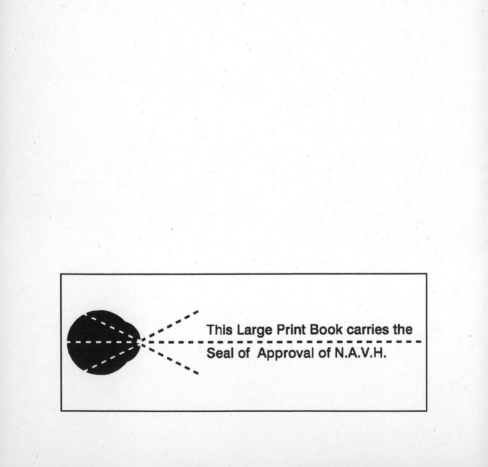

This Large Print Book carries the
Seal of Approval of N.A.V.H.

THE LAWSONS OF LOUISIANA

WHEN I'M WITH YOU

DONNA HILL

THORNDIKE PRESS
A part of Gale, a Cengage Company

Farmington Hills, Mich • San Francisco • New York • Waterville, Maine
Meriden, Conn • Mason, Ohio • Chicago

LIBRARY OF CONGRESS CIP DATA ON FILE.
CATALOGUING IN PUBLICATION FOR THIS BOOK
IS AVAILABLE FROM THE LIBRARY OF CONGRESS

ISBN-13: 978-1-4328-6073-8 (hardcover)

Published in 2019 by arrangement with Harlequin Books S.A.

Printed in Mexico
1 2 3 4 5 6 7 23 22 21 20 19

Dear Reader,

Thank you for joining me on another peek behind the scenes of the Lawson family. In *Surrender to Me,* Rafe Lawson, bad-boy heir to the Lawson fortune, was finally snared by a woman who was his equal, Secret Service agent Avery Richards. Of course, their road to happiness had its obstacles, but together they fought their way through. Now, in the only sequel to The Lawsons of Louisiana series, Rafe is back and ready to walk down the aisle — but not without his past coming back to change everything.

Rafe Lawson is definitely one of my favorite male characters. I so enjoyed giving him that "edge," that inaccessibility, but at the same time having him be a complex character who is much deeper than what he appears on the surface.

When I decided to write *When I'm with You,*

part two of his life, I knew that there had to be some bombshells that needed to be dropped, and drop they do. Rafe will be tested in a way that he has never been tested before, and Avery must decide if the Rafe Lawson that she fell in love with is the man she can anchor her future to, even as she struggles with her own secrets.

When I'm with You is a testament to what it means when a man loves a woman and a woman loves him back. Savor each page. Root for true love. Enjoy!

Until next time,
Donna

ACKNOWLEDGMENTS

Big thanks to all of my readers new and old that have made The Lawsons of Louisiana series such a success.

I couldn't do it without you.

CHAPTER 1

"Your sisters are planning *our* wedding," Avery said as she loaded the dishwasher.

Rafe handed her the glasses from the table. "Yeah, they can be a bit enthusiastic," he said chuckling. He came up behind her, bent over her body and grabbed her waist. "The main thing is we're going to be legal, official, permanent."

Avery straightened and turned to face him, leaned against the dishwasher. She looked into his eyes, and as always a flood of heat flowed through her. Being in the same air space with Rafe always did that to her, made her hungry for him, weak to his will. But this was *her* wedding, *her* day. She splayed her hands against his chest. "Look, babe, I know it's your family, and I don't want to cause any rifts, but . . . I need some space."

Rafe's simmering gaze slowly moved over her face, the way it did whenever he was trying to see beneath the surface of her words. She shifted her weight under his close scrutiny.

"I'll talk to them, okay," he said softly.

Avery pressed her lips together and nodded her head.

"Come 'ere." He pulled her tight against him. "All I want is for you to be happy. Just tell me what you want and I'll make it happen."

Avery rested her head against his chest, soothed by the steady beat of his heart. Her temple suddenly pounded and a flash of sharp pain shot across her eyes. Her body tensed.

Rafe eased back and looked down at her taut expression. "You okay? Another headache?" He stroked her cheek.

Avery let out a slow breath. "A little. It'll pass."

Since the explosion in Paris and the concussion she sustained when she'd rescued Rafe's father, she'd intermittently suffered from mild to severe headaches. The doctors assured her that they would lessen and then eventually disappear with time.

"Maybe we need to get the doctor to run some more tests."

"No." She shook her head. "It's only been a little over two months."

"Yes, but you go back to work next week. The doctor has to clear you. You have to be on your A-game, darlin'. You said so yourself."

She leaned up and kissed his lips. "And I will be." There was no way she would see any doctors and tell them what was really going on with her. They'd never clear her to return to duty. And if so it would be desk duty. She did not work her way up the ranks of the Secret Service to sit behind a desk. Plus, she was up for promotion. No way would she blow it. Two Advil. End of story. "I'm fine." She turned the dial on the dishwasher and it hummed to life. Another morning of domesticity.

After leaving Paris, Rafe took Avery to the Lawson compound to recuperate from her injuries before returning to Avery's place in Washington, DC. Rafe easily made her townhouse his second home. Their pseudo "living together" arrangement was easier than she'd imagined.

They were a natural fit with each other, as if living under the same roof was something they'd always done. Rafe was attentive, but gave her space. He possessed chef-like skills in the kitchen, a penchant for neatness — she never had to step over discarded clothing, or clean up after a meal — and above all he was a master in the bedroom who made her see heaven on a regular basis. This man was going to be her husband. Sometimes when she looked at him or held him tight between her thighs, she couldn't believe that Rafe Lawson was hers. What she wanted was just the two of them, but marrying Rafe was marrying his large, controlling family.

"You sure you'll be okay until I get back from 'Nawlins?" He wiped off the countertop with a damp cloth.

She shimmied onto the barstool at the island counter and extended her hands to Rafe. He took two long steps and was in front of her. He raised her hands to his lips and kissed the insides of her palms.

"I'll be fine, and right here when you get back." She leaned in to kiss him.

"Hmm, I can change my plans," he said against her cheek, "and stay here, which is what I'd rather do." He caressed her hips.

Avery giggled. "Me, too, but you've been gone long enough. Take care of your business."

He stepped deep between her legs. "Business can wait." He threaded his fingers through the hair at the nape of her neck, dipped his head and kissed her collarbone.

Avery sucked in a breath of desire and

instinctively tightened her legs around him. "You're going to be late," she whispered.

He brushed his lips along her neck, nibbled the lobe of her ear. "Privilege is the perk of owning your own plane. Can't leave without me." He covered her lips with his and drew her tongue into his mouth.

Avery untied the belt on her robe and then looped her arms around his neck. "Thank you for perks," she said, as Rafe lifted her from the stool. She wrapped her legs around his waist while he walked them into her bedroom.

Rafe eased her down on the bed and braced his weight above her. "Say the word, darlin'," he whispered in her ear while he stroked her hip and then lifted her left thigh and draped it over his arm, "and I'll stay." He nuzzled her neck, dipped his head down to suckle the peaks of her breasts.

Her heart raced. "Rafe . . ." she moaned.

"Tell me what you want." He slid his hands beneath her and pushed deep inside.

"Ahhh . . ." She clung to him. "You . . . only you."

"You got me. Always," he said from between his teeth and let his body prove it.

"I can drive you to the airport," Avery dreamily offered as she stretched her naked

13

body beneath the twisted pale blue sheets.

Rafe glanced over his shoulder, lifted the sheet and peeked underneath. "Naw, darlin', this is how I want to remember you while I'm gone." He lightly swatted her lush bottom and pushed up off the bed. "Gonna shower and dress. Want anything while I'm up?"

"Hmm," she moaned. "Nope." She tugged the sheet up to her chin and closed her eyes.

Rafe chuckled and padded off to the bathroom.

Avery distantly heard the rush of shower water, soon followed by Rafe's rendition of The Temptations' "My Girl." She smiled and burrowed into the overstuffed pillow. How would she manage without Rafe? They spent their days talking, debating, laughing, investing in each other's happiness, and their nights consummating their love. This would be the first time they'd be apart . . . since Paris . . .

The scent of smoke filled her nostrils. Her heart raced. *Blackness. Screams. Pain. Sirens.* The sheets clung to her damp body. Sinking. She was sinking. Falling. Had to get out.

"Avery!" Rafe gently clasped her shoulder and sat next to her on the bed. "Cher . . ."

Her eyes flew open. Her body trembled.

14

Rafe gathered her up in his arms. "Sssh, just a dream, cher." He rocked and held her until the shaking stopped.

"I'm ok-aay." She forced a smile and pushed her damp hair away from her face.

"No, you're not. And I'm not going anywherc. Not leaving you."

Avery pushed herself into a sitting position. "I'm fine, Rafe. Really. Just a dream — like you said. The doctors said to expect flashbacks. That's all it was. Period." She took his face in her hands. "If it will make you feel better, I'll ask Kerry to stay over until you get back."

A deep line etched itself between sleek, dark brows. "No. Kerry has to work. You'll be alone all day."

"Rafe, it's just a headache and some bad dreams. I'm not an invalid."

"I'll go on one condition only." He looked hard into her eyes.

She folded her arms and pouted. "What?"

"You stay at my house in Arlington. Alice is there. She can get you whatever you need, keep you company."

"You mean keep tabs on me," she said with an arched brow.

"Well, yeah. That, too," he conceded with that slow smile.

Avery huffed, pondered the offer. "Okay.

15

If that's what it's gonna take to get you on that plane."

"That's exactly what it's gonna take. I'll call and let Alice know to stock up. Make a list of anything special you want and I'll let her know." He pointed a finger at her. "List. Pack." He winked and then turned to get his clothes and dress.

By the time he'd finished dressing, Avery was ready to get into the shower. She'd left a list on the bed. Rafe grinned. Martini mix and taco fixings. He placed a call to Alice and let her know company was coming. Alice was delighted that Avery would be staying at the house and promised to take great care of her while he was gone.

"Got everything?" Rafe asked while he carried her bag to the door.

Avery stood in the middle of her living room and took a slow, deliberate look around. She drew in a deep breath. Every move that she'd made since she graduated high school was to establish independence. After she lost her mother in her teens and spent almost the next decade eating her way through life, before she hit her own near-life-or-death moment, she finally turned all her energy into gaining control over every aspect of her life — from healthy eating to religiously exercising, to a laser focus on rising up the ranks of the Secret Service. She cherished the life that she'd built for herself, *by herself,* even as her father worked tirelessly to keep her reined in.

This packing up and going to stay at Rafe's place, under his direction, went against every instinct of self-preservation that she had. She gritted her teeth. "I think so," she finally said. She hiked her oversize zebra-print tote over her shoulder, snatched up her keys from the table by the door and walked out. "What about my car?"

Rafe opened the passenger door to his Navigator and froze when he caught the look of panic in her eyes. He cupped her cheeks in his hands. "Cher," he crooned, "we'll take your car if you want, and leave mine here. I'll take a cab to the airfield."

The burn of tears threatened to spill. She blinked rapidly and nodded in agreement. "Thank you," she whispered.

He leaned down and gently kissed her lips. "I know, darlin'," he said in his easy drawl. "This isn't what you want. But I promise, it's going to be all right. Trust me." He lifted her chin and looked into her eyes. "Trust me."

Avery swallowed over the dry knot in her throat. "I do."

"Good." He shut the passenger door of

his Navigator, took her keys, walked around and opened her car door.

Avery tossed her tote on the back seat while Rafe stowed her bags in the trunk and then got in behind the wheel.

"Listen . . ." He buckled his seat belt. "I know you crave your space." He reached across the gearshift and took her hand. "All I want is to make sure you're okay. That you're safe. I'd make myself crazy in 'Nawlins worrying about you. I want to take care of you, cher. Let me," he added gently.

Avery leaned in and lightly kissed him. "I know . . . thank you . . . really."

He gave her a reflective look as he caressed her chin with his thumb. Then he turned the key in the ignition and pulled off.

Less than an hour later, Rafe eased Avery's car down the driveway of his Arlington, Virginia, home. He shut off the engine, just as Alice pulled the front door open and stepped out. She hurried over to the car.

"Mr. Rafe. So good to have you home. And Ms. Avery." She wrapped her arms around Avery in a motherly hug and buzzed her cheek with a kiss. "Come, come. Let's get you settled. Are you hungry?"

Avery giggled. "I'm fine, Alice. Thanks."

"I have everything all prepared. You can

stay in the guest room, or Mr. Rafe's room," she added with a wink and then led them inside. "And I made a tray of snacks just in case," she tossed over her shoulder.

Rafe glanced at Avery. The smile on her face eased the knot of tension in his gut. He slid an arm around her waist and they walked inside.

Avery held Rafe's hand that rested on her hip. "Thank you for this," she said.

"Nothing to thank me for." He squeezed her hip. "I want you to be taken care of. Anything you need, let Alice know." He grinned. "She loves taking care of people."

"Your car is here!" Alice called out.

"See." He grinned and kissed her forehead. "Sorry, darlin'. I need to get going. Want to beat this weather."

Avery looped her arm through his, and they walked out of his bedroom, downstairs and out to the car that waited to take him to the airport.

"I'll call you when I get in."

"Fly safe."

"Always." He kissed her lightly. "Love you." He glanced past her toward the house. "Take care of my woman," he called out to Alice, who stood on the front steps. He gave Avery one last hug. "Call you tonight."

Avery nodded and stepped back as he got in the car, before taking a quick look at the overcast sky.

The car door slammed, and the car slowly eased down the driveway and out to the street. Avery felt a rush of emptiness open inside her. A warm arm slid around her shoulders and held her close. Alice smiled knowingly up at her.

"Mr. Rafe will be fine, and back before you know it. Come inside. You must try my jambalaya! Just a little taste," she teased with a sparkle in her eyes.

"I'd love some."

"Oh. My. God. This is sooo good," Avery gushed, finishing off another mouthful.

Alice beamed. "Have as much as you like. There's plenty." She pulled out a chair and sat opposite Avery at the circular wrought-iron and reclaimed-wood table.

"I am so happy that Mr. Rafe finally settled down."

Avery glanced up from beneath her lashes.

"His heart was so broken . . . after Janae." She slowly shook her head. "I didn't think he would ever be the same." She turned her palms up. "And he's not," she said succinctly. "He's better." She wagged a finger at Avery. "Because of you."

"What . . . was he like after . . ."

Alice's open expression grew somber. Her brows tightened. She spread her palms down on the table. "Rafe was always a little wild and reckless, especially with that motorcycle of his. But after Janae, whatever piece of himself that kept him halfway grounded broke. On the outside, he was the same — that easy smile, the charm, the chivalry. But there was a darkness that settled inside him. He took crazy chances, went from relationship to relationship, in constant conflict with his father — more than usual. I was afraid for him. Every time he got behind the wheel, or on that bike or up in that plane of his, I prayed." She made a quick sign of the cross. "Because I knew, under that smile, he didn't care about his own life anymore."

"I had no idea," she murmured.

"I'd been with the family for years, but when Rafe decided to take over this house, I came here. He needed someone to look after him since he wasn't going to look after himself. Back in 'Nawlins, he has his sisters and brother."

"The move had to be hard on you."

"I've been taking care of Mr. Rafe and his family since they were running around in shorts. He's like a son to me." She lowered her voice as if she feared being overheard. "Always was my favorite." She winked.

Avery grinned.

"Then he met you and the light came back to his eyes. His laughter is real again and that . . . thing that drove him to be so reckless seems to have stepped into the background. He wants to be around for you."

Avery's throat tightened. "How'd you know I needed to hear this today?"

Alice patted Avery's fisted hand. "I haven't spent half my life taking care of people without being able to spot need in someone."

"I'm glad he has you in his life."

Alice pushed up to her feet. "Now that you're part of the family, I'll be looking after you, too. And I think you could use a hot bath, a fluffy robe and a good movie."

Avery tossed her head back and laughed. "You read my mind. Alice, can I ask you something?"

"Of course." She collected the plates.

"How do I get Dominique, Desiree and Lee Ann to . . . let me have my own wedding?"

Alice pursed her lips. "Hmm, those three sisters together are like a hurricane, with Dominique at the center of the storm." She

22

turned on the faucet in the sink, rinsed the plates and put them in the dishwasher. "They adore their brother, and they're so thrilled that he's happy again — they want to orchestrate every detail of the occasion for him." She dried her hands on a black-and-white striped towel, blew out a breath. "One piece of advice I can offer, you don't want to get in between Rafe and his sisters. If what they're doing is too much, talk to them. Make sure you're part of the plans and decisions. All of you women love him, so do it together."

Avery bobbed her head. "Thanks." She got up. "In the meantime, I'm going to take your advice and sit in a hot tub for a while."

Avery went upstairs. She searched the cabinet beneath the sink and located the bath beads that she'd brought over the last time she was here. She poured a handful into the water rushing into the tub from the jets. Although she took a shower earlier, the bath would be therapeutic. Almost immediately the scent of soothing lavender filled the room. She stripped out of her clothes, turned off the faucets and sank into the steamy, scented water.

Every muscle sighed in pleasure. She leaned her head back against the lip of the tub and closed her eyes. Alice's words of advice played softly. She didn't have the time or opportunity to go down to Louisiana to do a face-to-face with Rafe's sisters. She'd figure something out. She'd find a way to get them to accept that it was time to let Rafe go and that she would be part of his life and their family.

CHAPTER 2

Rafe disembarked from his Cessna. Flying always filled him with an awesome sense of invincibility. High above the clouds was a feeling that he could not describe. The only thing more thrilling was being with Avery. He smiled. He'd barely been gone three hours and he missed her already.

He thanked the crew, hopped on his motorcycle that he'd left parked at the landing strip and sped home. As he rode with a controlled abandon, the landscape of his life spread out before him. He'd spent years doing just this, racing through life, not taking the time to really see what was in front of him. Sure, there were good times to be had, and he'd never want to go back and change them. But he'd done it all while running on empty. For all the travel, the music gigs, the successes — and failures — and the women, there was a space inside him that none of those things could fill. He was starting to feel whole again from the inside. All the bourbon, reckless behavior, and even the fights with his father were all part of trying to fill the emptiness.

He maneuvered around a slow-moving minivan, resisting the urge to lean in and press the gas all the way down to the blacktop of the highway. He smiled beneath the tinted visor that shielded his face. It was all Avery's fault. She was the one responsible for his reincarnation.

Rafe signaled for his exit, dutifully followed the flow of cars up the ramp and out into residential traffic. After a short ten-minute ride he pulled into the driveway of his two-story townhouse. The garage door whirred open. He parked his bike inside and entered the house through the door that led to the kitchen. He set his helmet on the granite countertop, tugged off the black leather gloves and tossed them there, as well.

He walked through the kitchen and into the living space to be greeted by the pile of mail that had been slid inside the mail slot of the front door. Scooping up the stack of bills, newspapers and subscription magazines, he absently sorted through half of them, deciding what to keep and what to toss, before dropping them on the end table.

And then he headed upstairs to his bedroom.

He wanted to change his clothes first. After that he would get in touch with his producer to set up a meeting about the new tracks, and then check in with Quinten and try to twist his arm into coming to the Big Easy to sit in on a set. He'd bribe him with gumbo. Tomorrow he would go to the office. Although he'd put together a solid team for his foundation, he still needed to show his face and be a presence. Besides, there was something intangibly fulfilling about walking into a building and into rooms he'd envisioned that were now a reality. But it was the good work the RBL Foundation did for the young people of the community that was immeasurable. For all the crazy bull that he'd done in his life, the Foundation at least put a fresh coat of paint over it, and it was certainly an endeavor that he could be proud of.

He pulled on a pair of well-worn gray sweatpants and a T-shirt and then went back downstairs in search of food. Passing through the living room he grabbed the mail he'd tossed on the end table and took it with him to the kitchen.

Although the Lawson family always had a housekeeper, each of the Lawson siblings learned how to cook. And if Rafe had to say so himself, he was pretty damned good. He tugged open the fridge. Milk, eggs, a half roll of salami and something in a plastic bowl that he didn't recognize. The trick of course was to remember to shop. He pulled open the vegetable bin and grinned with relief at the sight of a green and a red pepper that still had life in them, along with a package of shredded cheddar cheese. Omelet coming right up.

While he wolfed down his omelet, he snapped open one of the major New Orleans newspapers that he received via delivery service. He started at the back of the paper, in the sports section, worked his way forward and nearly choked on his omelet when a picture of him and Avery — taken when he had no idea — with the caption "Rafe Lawson, New Orleans's most eligible bachelor, engaged to Avery Richards." There was a short paragraph that followed, announcing the engagement and that Avery was the daughter of Senator Horace Richards. It went on to state that the marriage of Lawson and Richards will redefine the political power couple. The nuptials are scheduled for early summer. No date has been set.

With every word, the knot in his stomach tightened. First of all, where the hell did anyone get their picture? Were they being followed? And most important, who gave the damned newspaper information on his and Avery's engagement? He slapped the paper down on the counter. Had to be one of his sisters, and he would bet money that it was Dominique. It had her signature all over it.

"Shit." He pushed back from the table with such force that the stool toppled backward, hit the floor and rolled. He gripped the paper in his fist and stormed upstairs to get dressed. His visit to the family home was going to be sooner rather than later.

Friday nights when the family was in town they generally turned up at the family home at some point. Hopefully tonight would be no different, which would help him avoid having to make a round of house calls. More than likely Lee Ann was in DC with Sterling. And he didn't think the announcement in the paper was her doing, anyway.

Rafe opted to drive his Audi. As furious as he was he didn't want to get on the road with his bike. He checked the trunk to make sure his small duffel bag with his "on the road" change of clothing was inside. He unzipped the bag and did a quick check of the contents. Satisfied, he slammed the trunk shut and got in behind the wheel. He had a very strong feeling that tonight would be a three-bourbon evening and driving would not be an option.

Halfway between his home and the family residence Rafe used the voice-activated phone feature and called Avery.

"Hi, darlin'," he said the moment the call connected.

"Hi." She yawned.

"Everything good? Sounds like I woke you."

"Hmm, I guess I really did nod off. Alice fed me and insisted I take a hot bath." She yawned again. "I thought I was reading," she said over light laughter.

Rafe chuckled. "Not going to keep you. You need your rest. Just wanted to hear your voice and let you know I got here okay."

"Sounds like you're outside or something."

"Yeah, I'm on my way to the family house."

"Oh."

"Plan to talk to my sisters . . . about the wedding." No reason to tell her more than that. He'd deal with the mess in the papers.

Alice's advice rushed to the forefront. "Rafe . . . babe, I was being overly sensitive. I'm not going to put you in between me and your family. When I come down there next month I can talk to them myself. I know they mean well."

Rafe ran his tongue across his bottom lip. He couldn't let it go. It wasn't in his DNA, but he wasn't going to upset Avery. "Whatever you want to do, darlin'. As long as you're happy and stress-free. To me, that's what's important."

"Thanks. Well, say hello to the fam for me."

"I will."

"Love you."

"You, too, cher. I'll call you tomorrow."

"Okay. Have a good evening."

"You, too."

The call disconnected. Rafe frowned. He didn't want to slip into a habit of lying to Avery. Even though what he told her wasn't an out-and-out lie, it was a lie by omission. If he could stomp out the newspaper reports, then she wouldn't have to know. His line of reasoning was thin to say the least. What he needed to do, in the meantime, was set his sisters straight. The last thing he wanted was for Avery to get bombarded with her face plastered on the tabloids and splashed across every Louisiana paper's gossip section. He was used to it. He grew up on the receiving end of razor-sharp pens and intrusive flashbulbs, lived much of his adult life as a "trending topic" and grew immune to seeing his face on the pages of the news or covers of magazines. But that wasn't Avery's life. He had to do everything in his power to protect her. She may carry a gun and have security clearances, but both were useless against vigilant and determined journalists.

Rafe made the turn onto the private grounds where the Lawson mansion stood, glad to see some lights on, signaled right and eased his vehicle down the winding road that opened onto the sweeping green landscape that braced the eight-bedroom, six-bath family home. Growing up, it was nothing to play hide-and-seek in the massive house, peek into the formal dining room to see the famous faces of those that most only saw on television, slide down the mahogany bannisters, race for hours across the grassy lawn, attend the best schools or skip rocks along the pond that ran behind the house. For him and his siblings, and cousins that frequented the home, it was all pretty normal. But his father and his uncles drilled into them from the time that they were old enough to sit still and listen that the life the Lawsons lived was a privilege, not a right, and as such they owed society a debt, and that debt was to pay it forward. Each of his siblings, minus himself and Dominique, embraced the Lawson mantra. As the two rebels of the family, Rafe and Dominique were hell-bent and determined to do whatever was necessary to tick their father off. Their track record in that regard was impeccable. Dominique should have been his twin instead of Desiree's. He and Dom were true sibling soulmates. However, that pesky thing called love swept through the Lawson clan like a summer storm and took each of them out one by one, Dominique included. Rafe remained the last holdout — until Avery.

He parked on the side of the house, used his key to open the front door. The aroma of backyard barbecuing mixed with laughter beckoned him. He followed the lip-smacking scents and was met by the wide-eyed surprise of his aunt Jacqueline, his brother Justin and his fiancée, Bailey.

"Rafe!" Jacqueline greeted him, her smile wide. "I thought you were in DC, baby."

"Hey, big bro," Justin said, raising a bottle of beer in salute.

Rafe rounded the white wrought-iron table, leaned down and gave his aunt a hearty kiss on the cheek. "Hey, Aunt J, good to see you. Where's Ray?"

Raymond Jordan had long been his aunt's freelance photographer. They'd traveled the world together, chasing that elusive story in some of the most exotic and often dangerous places on the globe. Finally they realized that what they needed — beyond the excitement of the next assignment — was each other. More than that, Raymond was instrumental in seeing his aunt through one of the most difficult times in her life. As much as her brother Branford's bone marrow saved her body, Raymond's love saved her soul. Now that the Lawson children were either married off or working on it, the house for the most part was empty. Jacqueline and Raymond decided to return to Jacqueline's childhood home and finally put down some roots.

Jacqueline laughed at her nephew's question. "Down in the wine cellar. He swears he's a wine expert now."

Rafe chuckled and went to bear-hug his brother. "Hey, bro. Didn't expect to see you here. When did ya'll get in?"

"Came in from New York this morning. Just for the weekend."

Rafe turned to his sister-in-law-to-be. "Bailey, woman, you still hanging out with this guy," he teased and buzzed her cheek.

Bailey giggled. "No other choice. He's

stuck with me."

Justin draped his arm around Bailey's shoulder and winked up at his brother.

"You two keep it up and somebody's gonna write a book about you," Rafe playfully warned.

"Very funny," Justin groused. "But I see you're still in the headlines." He lifted his chin toward a magazine tossed on top of the side table.

Rafe's eyes narrowed and zeroed in on the magazine.

"My man," came a hearty greeting from behind Rafe.

Rafe looked over his shoulder. Raymond stepped out onto the veranda with a bottle of wine in each hand.

"Now it's a party," Raymond joked and set the bottles down on the table.

Rafe grinned. "Was just asking about you. Looking good, man."

"Other than the snowcaps," he said, running a hand over his head and then stroking his tapered goatee, "I'm feeling good." He patted his chiseled belly. "Gotta keep up with my gorgeous wife."

"How's Avery doing?" Bailey asked.

"She's good," Rafe said on a breath. "Heading back to work next week."

"So soon," Jacqueline said with a frown.

She held out her flute, which Raymond filled with chilled red wine. "Seems like that mess in France was just the other day," she softly said and mouthed her thanks to Raymond, who took a seat next to her. "Your father is still recovering. Still needs a cane to get around and rehab once per week."

"Dad's injuries were a little more severe, Aunt J. He had broken bones, *and* he's no kid."

"Still . . ." She sipped her wine. "As long as she's better."

The headaches, the nightmares . . . The family didn't need to know all that. "Yeah, me too." He stepped around his brother and pulled up a chair from the back end of the veranda.

"Beer's in the cooler," Justin offered.

"Thanks." He flipped open the cooler and took out a can and then reached for the magazine. His jaw tightened. There was a picture of him holding open a car door for Avery, with the caption "Louisiana playboy Rafe Lawson a person of interest to Secret Service Agent Avery Richards." He muttered a string of curses under his breath. "You wanted to know what brought me here," he ground out, flashing a look at his aunt. "That's why." He tossed the offending magazine onto the table.

"Guess you haven't seen the local daily paper," Justin said with a raised brow. "Big spread."

Rafe's jaw tightened.

"Rafe," Jacqueline began, her tone soft and entreating. "You know how this works, especially with our family."

"*I* do. But Avery doesn't."

"Maybe not, but unfortunately when she agreed to marry you it came with all the Lawson baggage. Media has been tracking your every move since you were a teenager."

"Gotta admit, big bro, you always give them plenty to feed on," Justin added.

And now Avery was paying for his wild ways. Rafe pushed out a breath and plopped down in the available chair, stretched his long legs out in front of him. He snapped off the top of the beer and took a long, deep swallow. "Yeah," he muttered in reluctant agreement. "Pictures are one thing, but giving details is something else."

"What do you mean?" Bailey asked.

"Announcements in the papers about our engagement. Someone had to tell them, and it wasn't me."

Everyone got quiet.

Rafe looked from one averted face to the next. "Dominique," he said for all of them. He shook his head.

"You know Dom," Jacqueline offered, stretching out her hand to cover his. "She's so happy for you and Avery. Making the announcement wasn't done to hurt you."

"I know."

"Your wedding is all she talks about."

Rafe sighed. He knew his family was sincerely happy that he was finally settling down, that he'd found someone to fill the space in his life. After Janae, he'd gone on a buck-wild, non-stop binge of reckless living. When he met Avery, his world finally came into focus and his nonchalant attitude shifted. He finally, for the first time in years, wanted more than the thrill of the moment. He wanted a forever. His aunt and brother were right, of course. He'd lived his life, along with the rest of his family, under the glare of the spotlight. However, it was a part of his reality that he didn't want for Avery, especially when the glare of the spotlight was intentional. Add the zeal of his sisters into the mix, wanting to have their hands in every aspect of the wedding, and it was a blowup waiting to happen. As much as he may not have a problem with his sisters planning his wedding, his first obligation now was to Avery. She was the only one he wanted to make happy. Dominique was going to have to take a step back. Two steps.

"Dom coming by this weekend?" Rafe asked.

"Probably," Jacqueline said. "I was planning Sunday dinner. She usually drops by."

Rafe nodded. He pushed up from the chair and stood. "In the meantime, what's a brotha gotta do to get some of that barbecue?"

The tense air filled with relieved laughter.

"That's what I'm talkin' 'bout," Raymond said.

Rafe walked over to the stainless-steel grill that was set up outside of the veranda. *Sunday couldn't get here fast enough.* He loaded a plate with ribs and a side of salad to take the edge off. He and Dominique were going to have a serious chat.

CHAPTER 3

Avery slipped on the pale peach satin robe, which Rafe purchased for her on one of their spontaneous vacations, and went downstairs to the kitchen.

"Good morning!" Alice greeted her with a broad smile. "You look rested."

"Good morning. Yes, I am. Hmm, something smells delicious."

"Cheese grits, maple-dipped bacon and light-as-a-feather eggs. I wasn't sure when you would be getting up. But everything is in the warmer. Fresh coffee and juice. Take as much as you want. I need to run some errands in a bit, but I should be back in an hour or two."

"Sure. Go."

"Do you need anything?"

"No. I'm fine. Thanks." She pulled out a chair from the breakfast nook and sat down, while Alice slipped out of the kitchen and took care of all the magic she created in the house. The silver warming tray, and a glass bowl of chopped fresh fruit was in the center of the table. Avery lifted the oblong cover of the warming tray and smiled. She had to admit, it would be really easy to get used to this kind of life. She scooped eggs, bacon and grits onto her plate and added fresh fruit.

A copy of *The Washington Post* lay neatly folded at the end of the table. She pulled it closer and then poured herself a mug of coffee.

The front page was plastered with raw images of the devastation across the Caribbean islands and Puerto Rico that were still recovering, months later, from a series of catastrophic hurricanes that ravished the areas. A wave of sadness swept through her. She could not begin to imagine what the people continued to go through. Meanwhile, here at home, the country was not being torn apart by outside forces, but from those within.

She slowly chewed her food and flipped the pages, scanning the headlines, from international news to arts and entertainment. She choked at the shock of seeing her face staring back at her from the paper and then grabbed a glass of juice to wash down the bacon.

Avery's pulse quickened. It was a picture of her and Rafe at that outdoor café they loved in DC. Beneath it was a caption and a short paragraph, announcing their engagement and pending summer wedding. They were at that café shortly before she went off on detail to Paris, *before* the engagement. Her thoughts turned in circles. *She* certainly wasn't anyone a journalist would be interested in. If anything, because of her work she remained as low-key and inconspicuous as possible. She dropped the paper down on the table. It wasn't her they were photographing; it was Rafe, and she was swept up in the tide of his notoriety even outside of Louisiana. Collateral damage.

Having his sisters orchestrate her wedding was difficult enough to navigate, but this kind of publicity could jeopardize her job, more important, put at risk the people she was sworn to protect.

"Dammit!" She pushed away from the table. This was going to turn into a nightmare. She felt it in the pit of her stomach and she had no idea what to do about it.

"I just saw it," Kerry said into the phone. "Are you okay?"

"I don't know, girl. I'm stuck between stunned that the rest of the world gives a

42

damn who I marry, to furious that the rest of the world gives a damn." She pushed out a breath of frustration. "It was bad enough when my own father had me followed when me and Rafe first started dating. At least I could get him to stop with his craziness. This is a whole other story and I have no idea how this is going to play out at work."

"Hmmm, yeah, there's that. But, hey, no way is the Secret Service going to allow photographers to trail around, taking pictures."

Avery let her head flop back against the cushion of the couch. "I guess," she muttered.

"If it helps any I haven't heard any whisperings or gossip here at work."

"That's good, and I want it to stay that way."

"Listen . . . I know how you are about privacy. It's part of our job, but it's also part of who you are. I know you. If you could move through the day without having to give over anything of yourself, you would. I get that your self-imposed isolation is a defense mechanism. If no one can get close, no one can hurt you. But now there's Rafe."

Even the sound of his name made her heart tumble in her chest.

"What you have going with Rafe is a

whole new world for you. You're going to have to find a way to deal with it, sis, if you want to marry him."

"I know," she whispered. "I just wish . . . it was the two of us, ya know. He has this big-ass family . . ."

"Try to look at it this way, you'll finally have not only a husband but a *real* family, Avery, with sisters and brothers and cousins. You won't be that motherless, only child anymore. Embrace it, instead of trying to keep it like a side chick." They both laughed at her comparison. "You deserve a family," she added softly.

It was true. She did deserve a family, although she had no idea what being part of one even meant. After her mother died, with no siblings or extended family, it was her and her father, Horace. Rather it was *her.* Horace Richards turned his entire life toward building his career in politics. She was on her own. Kerry was the closest thing to family that she had . . . until Rafe.

"I'll try," she conceded. "Anyway, stop by when you get off."

"His place is out in Arlington, right?"

"On second thought, I need to get out of the house. Why don't we meet for dinner? I can drive in."

"Sounds like a plan."

"Seven?"

"Works for me."

"Let's meet up at Baldwin's. We haven't been there in a minute." Baldwin's, named in honor of literary icon James Baldwin, was renowned for its excellent cuisine, but especially for the literati who frequented the establishment, often reading from their new works, performing spoken word or just chilling. The vibe was stimulating while simultaneously relaxing.

"Perfect. See you there."

"Bye." Avery disconnected the call and set the phone down on the table. She glanced around. What was she going to do with herself for the rest of the day? Maybe she'd go for a run, burn off some of her pent-up energy, clear her head.

She pushed up from the couch and went into the bedroom to change clothes.

"Alice," she called out from the front door. "I'm going for a short run. Be back soon."

"Sure." She peeked her head out from the kitchen. "Should I fix lunch?"

Avery opened the front door. "Only if you promise to eat with me."

Alice smiled. "Okay."

"Great. Be back soon — in about an hour or so."

Avery stepped out into the bright afternoon. A light breeze blew, perfect for running. She did a few light stretches, started off and never noticed the car parked across the street.

Baldwin's, as always for a Saturday night, sizzled with energy. Music from the house's jazz band played their rendition of " 'Round Midnight," beckoning every customer who walked through the door to bob his or her head to the rhythm.

Avery could see from peeking around the tinted windows that separated the seated guests from the hostess station, that there were barely any empty tables. There were two sets of customers ahead of her and Kerry waiting to be seated: a couple and a party of four. Hopefully the wait wouldn't be too long.

Baldwin's, beyond the cultural significance of honoring the author, activist and icon James Baldwin, held a special place in her heart. On one of several visits when Rafe visited her in DC, Baldwin's was one of the venues where she heard him play. Was it that night that she fell irrevocably in love with him when he played Coltrane's "Love Supreme" to a standing ovation?

Kerry nudged her.

Avery blinked. "What?"

"What are you grinning about?"

"Oh," she laughed lightly, amused that she was caught in her daydream. "Just thinking about one of the nights I was here with Rafe."

"Table for two?" the hostess asked.

"Yes. Thank you," Kerry answered.

She took two menus from the holder on the podium and handed them off to a waitress. "Mia will show you to your seats."

Avery and Kerry walked several steps behind Mia as they wound their way around the dark circular tables, which were topped with white linen and illuminated by votive-candle centerpieces. The space, which was reputed to be one of the Underground Railroad passages, was rife with alcoves, thick cedar-wood rafters, plank floors and carvings in the wood walls, which urban legend claimed are the names and dates of slaves who had escaped — a testament to their passage. Each area of the two-story restaurant was designated as music, art, science, law, literature and named after a noted black figure, like Sojourner Truth, Nat Turner, Thurgood Marshall, Toni Morrison, Dr. King, Malcolm, Ida B. Wells, Gil Scott Heron, Sonia Sanchez, of course Baldwin and many others. Periodically, the management would switch out a namesake and replace it with another noted figure. On the tabletops, along with the candles, were tent cards with writings from the icons. Coming to Baldwin's was always an experience, as well as a mini lesson on the wealth of black history.

Tonight, Avery and Kerry were seated in the Thurgood Marshall section, which was off to the right of the stage, but still with great views of the comings and goings of the space.

Avery and Kerry settled in their seats and Mia took their drink orders, promising to be back shortly.

"I've been looking forward to this all day," Avery admitted. She flipped open the menu. "Yes, crab cakes!"

Kerry chuckled but then suddenly stopped.

Avery glanced up from the menu and landed on Mike, who was walking toward their table. She laid the menu flat.

"Avery . . . my God." His dark brown eyes widened in genuine surprise, followed by a smile that was actually warm. He took it upon himself, pulled out the extra chair and sat. He leaned in toward Avery. "How are you?" he asked, his voice low and insistent.

Tonight, Avery desperately wanted to get

away from everything that reminded her of Paris and what happened. Mike was a big reminder. They were both on duty the day of the explosion. When she came to, debris and bodies were everywhere. Mike was hurt during the blast. Her training kicked in and she began aiding the injured, one of them being Rafe's father, another was Mike, among the dozen or so others. She and Mike had their standoffs during their time at the Secret Service, both personal and professional, and were both up for the same promotion. Ironic that Mike should be right as rain and she was . . .

"Good to see you, too, Mike," Avery finally said.

"Word on the street is that you'll be back this week. True?"

"True."

He nodded. "It'll be good to have you back, Avery. Really."

"Thanks, Mike."

"Well, good to see you. You, too, Kerry."

Kerry umm-hmmed in her throat.

"Enjoy your evening." He got up and walked away.

Kerry reached across the table and covered Avery's fisted hand with her own. "You okay?"

Avery nodded. "Fine." She pushed out a

breath. "Going to have to get back to dealing with Mike sooner or later."

"I still can't believe that with all you went through, the heroics not to mention the injuries that you sustained, that Mike is even in the running for the promotion." Kerry shook her head in disbelief.

"You know as well as I do that this is an old-boys' club. The fact that women are part of the club at all, *and* rising up the ranks, still ticks off a lot of the establishment. If they can find anything to disqualify me, they will."

Mia returned with their drinks and took their dinner order.

Kerry raised her glass. "To kicking butt and taking names."

Avery tapped her glass against Kerry's. "All day." She took a long sip of her frozen strawberry margarita. She would not let anything or anyone stand in the way of getting what she rightly deserved, even if that meant lying to the doctors. No way would she stand down and let Mike walk in the shoes that should be hers. She picked up the tent card and read the inscription. It was a quote from Thurgood Marshall. "A man can make what he wants of himself if he truly believes that he must be ready for

hard work and many heartbreaks." Exactly,
and she was ready.

CHAPTER 4

Even after all the time that had gone by, and Miami, Florida, had become her home for the past sixteen years, she still kept up with the news from Louisiana and DC, and of course New York City, from her online subscriptions. It helped in her ongoing recovery to read about things that were once so familiar to her. There were still, even now, parts of her life that she could not distinguish between reality or a false memory. But the one thing she knew for certain was that she had been deeply and irrevocably in love. Now *he* was in love with someone else, marrying someone else.

His smile still made her soul shift, her heart beat just a little faster. She ran her finger across his face on her computer screen. He looked happy, truly happy . . . without her.

She lifted her hand and touched the scar that ran the length of her forehead, which she covered with bangs or innovative hair-styles. The burns she'd sustained on her legs had healed well, and were barely noticeable anymore. Some days when the pain was really bad she used a cane, but most of the time the medication the doctor prescribed worked.

She tilted her head to the side, studied the image from an angle. His fiancée was beautiful in an understated way. A part of her knew that she needed to let him and the past go. But the part of her that remembered what her life had been like with him wouldn't let her. He was the only thing from that time that she truly remembered. Them. The two of them against the world. The memory anchored her, kept her from losing the last vestiges of herself and falling into a dark hole of a manufactured past.

Sixteen years is enough time to move on. Rafe clearly did. She had for the most part. It was best — at least that's what her parents had told her. She'd believed them even though much of what their relation-ship had been was more mist than sub-stance. The fact that she'd survived at all was a miracle, the doctors said, and memory loss was the price that she paid for her survival. She'd done years of physical therapy, rounds of plastic surgery, seen countless specialists, but most of her life prior to that day was hazy at best. Except for Rafe Lawson. He was the only constant.

She longingly studied his picture before closing the cover of the computer. Much of what her life could have been was ripped from her, her body altered, her memory stolen. For years she'd been at the mercy of doctors and therapists and her parents, and bit by bit she began to create a new life. But she had to go back into the past. She owed it to herself and to Rafe. He loved *her* first and seeing her again would make him remember.

CHAPTER 5

Rafe returned to his Louisiana home, soothed somewhat by his aunt's calming words. She'd pulled him to the side shortly before he left to remind him that Dominique was his reflection and could have been his twin instead of Desiree's. Dom lived for excitement, upsetting the status quo and making a splash. Add in the fact that she adored her big brother and it was no surprise that she wanted the world to share her joy. Not to mention that Dominique Lawson thrived on attention, even if the attention was vicarious. He grabbed his go-bag from the trunk and carried it inside, thankful that he didn't have to use it. He shut the house door behind him, picked up the pile of mail he'd left on the table and turned on the lights against the overhanging gray of a new day. His aunt J was right. He and Dom were two sides of the same coin. He tugged off his jacket, tossed it on a side chair in the living room and dropped the mail on the couch, before turning on some music. Truth be told, the announcements and the pictures didn't really bother him, but they bothered Avery. So, somehow, he was going to have to get Dom to put a halt to her personal public-relations campaign, and for his sisters Lee Ann and Desiree to loosen the reins of wedding planning. And he had to do all that without starting WWIII. *Lucky me.*

He crossed the living room to the bar and fixed a shot of bourbon and then flopped back on the couch. He took a deep swallow, leaned his head back and closed his eyes. On Sunday he would get with Dominique and straighten things out. End of that story. But he still had plenty of other business to handle now that he was home, and he intended to make a quick pit stop to New York to get with Q, since it was unlikely that he'd bring Muhammad to the mountain, before returning to Virginia.

A lot had been put on hold since Avery's and his father's injuries from the bombing in Paris. Even though his nightclub and his foundation had good people at the helm, he kept his hand in. Lack of oversight was the downfall of too many businesses, and he had no intention of letting his become a statistic.

He finished off his drink and went through a mental checklist of everything he needed to take care of in the next few days. One thing that nagged at him, and something that he and Avery never really discussed, was where they would live. His businesses were in Louisiana, but her job was in DC. He supposed it was an unspoken understanding that he would be the one to relocate. It was easier for him, of course. Didn't mean he had to like it.

He blew out a breath and stretched his arm to gather up the mail he'd dumped on the other end of the couch, flipped through the envelopes and relegated each to either take care of or ignore. He stopped halfway, tossed everything else aside as he stared for a moment at the embossed return address of which he was very familiar with — the family attorney. Or rather his father's attorney that the family used. How had he missed this?

Frowning, he turned the envelope over, ripped it open and pulled out the thick sheaf of folded papers. His head jerked back as he read the first page for the second time.

"What the hell . . ." His eyes ran over the words in utter disbelief and rising fury.

His father had always tried to control the

lives of his children no matter how old they were or how far away they moved. But this! He hurled a string of expletives, picked up his phone to call his father but stopped. This conversation deserved a stare-you-in-the-eye sit down.

He shoved the pages back in the envelope, got up and put it in his go-bag. After he took care of his business here at home and in New York, his father's office in DC would be his next stop. He pulled out his cell from his back pocket and swiped to his phone calls. He pressed the phone icon, leaned back and waited.

"Hey, darlin'."

"Hi! I'm just walking in the door."

"Oh. Okay. Go get settled. We can talk another time."

"No. It's fine."

He heard a door close. "Everything good?"

"Yes. Kerry and I went to Baldwin's tonight."

He chuckled. "Love that place. Who was on set tonight?"

"House band. What about you? How was your visit?"

"Went well." His gaze drifted to his bag and the envelope that stuck out. "Anyway, cher, you get yourself together. We'll talk tomorrow. I'm kinda beat."

"Okay. Tomorrow, then." She paused. "I love you."

"Love you, too, cher. No matter what. Rest well."

"I will."

Rafe pressed the icon to end the call and tossed the phone toward the far end of the couch.

CHAPTER 6

Generally, after talking with Rafe, she always felt better, secure, uplifted, everything but what she felt now. She slipped out of her robe, turned back the sheets and crawled under the covers. Something was wrong. She felt it in the tone of Rafe's voice. It wasn't what he said, but what he didn't.

Had he brought up her concerns about the wedding and it didn't go well? Had he gotten into it with his sisters? She should have told him not to say anything. She was a big girl and didn't need her husband-to-be running to her rescue. She was skilled in dealing with insurmountable obstacles. How difficult could three sisters be?

She turned on her side and switched off the nightstand lamp, but it was hours before she finally fell into an exhausted sleep.

Alice was busy in the kitchen when Avery wandered in close to noon.

"Well, well, there you are." She wiped down the counter with a damp cloth. "You were up late."

Avery plopped down on a counter chair. "Couldn't sleep after I got in last night. Thought watching television would help. Sorry if I kept you up."

"Not at all. I'm a night owl. Came down to make some warm milk and I saw the television light on under your door." She came to stand beside Avery's hunched form. "Are you feeling okay? You don't look like yourself."

Avery forced a smile. "Who do I look like?" she teased.

Alice placed a comforting hand on Avery's stiff shoulder. "Like a woman who needs to talk." She sat down.

Avery blinked rapidly. She lowered her head and then glanced briefly at Alice. The only female in her life that she'd confided in was Kerry. Growing into womanhood without her mom, there was a reluctance inside that kept her from forming any female bonds for fear that the bond would be broken, taken from her like her mother was. She had no frame of reference for mothering, even as she desperately craved it.

Tears, unbidden, slid from her eyes.

Instinctively, Alice gathered Avery in her arms and held her close, let her cry. Tenderly she stroked her back and cooed soft words into Avery's hair. "Let it out," she soothed. "It's all right."

"I'm s-orry," Avery whispered and sniffed.

"Nothing to be sorry for. We all need a good cry every now and then."

Avery sniffed harder, wiped her eyes with the back of her hand and lowered her head.

Alice eased back but kept her hands planted on Avery's shoulders. "Want to tell me what's bothering you?" she gently asked.

Avery pushed out a long breath. "I don't know how to handle being in this family, any family. I've had to go at it on my own for most of my life. Then there's my career. It's all about orders and following instructions, being on alert, suspicious." She sighed. "In my life outside of work it's the only time when I can pull away from the straitjacket of my everyday life. Now, with the wedding and Rafe's family . . . all of those mixed feelings and experiences tumble all over each other and I don't know how to deal with it."

Alice patted Avery's thigh. "When you spend hours out of your day being on alert, looking for shadows in every corner, it's got to be hard to let that go, to trust that there are folks that ain't the boogeyman, that don't intend to hurt you, that only want to get close because they really do care. Rafe loves you and you love him, and he's not going to see you struggle against the weight of his overbearing family." She wagged a finger. "At the same time, you gonna have to dig deep and find a space that you can open." She smiled. "Burdens and troubles ain't so heavy when you have help." She tipped her head to the side. "How many weddings you planned?"

Avery's eyes widened. Her mouth opened a bit but then closed.

"Hmm. Those girls, if they know nothing else it's how to put a wedding together." She chuckled. "Give them and yourself a chance. I understand the ties that bind you at work. You don't get to speak up, only take orders, and it's hard to break old habits. But . . . how 'bout this. Next time, *you* initiate the get-together. *You* call Dom or Desi and tell them your thoughts. One step at a time?" Her right brow lifted with emphasis.

Avery pushed out a breath. "You're right. This is all so new to me."

"As much as those Lawsons may fuss and feud with each other, the love and the bond that they have is unbreakable." She squeezed Avery's hands. "They want you to be part

63

of that. And if you give it a chance, you might find what you've spent your life looking for."

Avery wiped away the remnants of her tears and offered up a wobbly smile. "I'll try."

Alice winked. "Good girl. Now," she planted her hands on her hips, "hungry?"

She smiled for real this time. "Starved."

CHAPTER 7

Avery finished her late breakfast, took a shower and went for a short run. She pushed through the stiff breeze wrapped in muggy air. Before she'd gone a little more than a block her skin grew damp and a line of perspiration dribbled down the center of her spine. Her limbs pumped. The fuel of adrenaline rushed through her veins, and clarity pushed through the cobwebs of her thoughts.

She loved Rafe. There was no doubt about that. Yes, she was overwhelmed by the rush of family, even a little scared. But if what Alice said was true, they wanted her to be part of who they were. She'd never had that before, but because she wanted a life with the man of her dreams she would find a way to work through her issues.

Avery rounded the corner and headed back to the house. Just as she slowed in front of the walkway, a car door opened and a man got out, blocking her path.

"Avery Richards, right?"

Her senses leapt to high alert. Instinctively her hand flew to her waist, where her gun would have been.

"Whoa!" He held up his hands. "Reporter."

She frowned. "Reporter? What do you want?" Her nostrils flared.

"I was hoping I could get a statement from you."

"I don't give statements." She tried to move, and he stepped into her path.

Her body flexed. "Step aside."

"I was hoping you would give me a comment about your engagement to Rafe Lawson. Your father is Horace Richards, right? Senator Richards."

Her head snapped to the right. "What did you say?" She took a step toward him and he flinched.

"Look, all I want is an exclusive for the paper. Playboy Lawson and heir to the family jewels hooks up with a senator's daughter — a Secret Service agent — that's news."

"Get away from me." This time she shoved him out of her way and started up the walkway.

"Are you staying here now? Have you moved in?" he shouted to her back.

Avery quickened her step, a beat short of a jog until she reached the front door. She took a quick look over her shoulder. The reporter snapped her picture. She opened the door and shut it solidly behind her. She leaned her back against it, felt her heart hammer in her chest.

Alice was walking toward her with a blue cloth shopping bag in her hand. She stopped halfway. "What is it?"

Avery vigorously shook her head. "Nothing. That run took more out of me than I thought."

Alice hurried over. "Go in and sit down. I'll get you some cold water."

Avery forced a smile. "Thanks. That's probably what I need."

Alice went off to the kitchen. Avery pulled herself together and walked out onto the back deck. Now she was being followed by reporters? How in the hell did they know where she . . . of course, the papers announcing the engagement. She pushed out a breath of frustration and squeezed her eyes shut for a moment. This was not good. The last thing she needed was to be followed around by reporters or photographed while she was on duty. Dammit!

Alice pushed open the screen door to the deck. "Here you go, sweetheart." She extended the glass of ice water toward Avery.

"Thanks, Alice." She took several long swallows before setting the glass down on the circular wrought-iron table.

Alice studied her for a moment. "Feeling better?"

Avery nodded. "Yes. Thanks."

"Okay. Well, I have my daily errands to run. Shouldn't take too long. Need anything while I'm out?"

Her thoughts swam. "Um, no. Thanks, Alice."

Alice turned and went back inside.

Avery lowered herself onto one of the lounge chairs. What was she going to do? Rafe felt it best that she stay in his home so that she wouldn't be alone. But clearly his house was being staked out. If there was one reporter, eventually there would be others. Going home might not be a better option. They probably knew where she lived.

She headed up to the bedroom, pulled out her suitcase and began to pack. Then she called Kerry.

CHAPTER 8

Avery checked the bedroom. Satisfied that she hadn't overlooked anything she shut the door and pulled her small rolling suitcase behind her. She made a quick stop in the kitchen to leave the note she'd written for Alice.

She took the extra set of keys that Rafe gave her and locked the door behind her. When she'd insisted that he drive her car to his house, it was more a matter of trying to maintain some sense of control. She turned the key in the ignition. Now it was her method of escape.

A little more than a half hour later she pulled up in front of Kerry's house and parked on the street. She stared at the house. What was she doing? She wasn't a runner. She didn't run from problems to avoid confrontations. Guess there was a first time for everything. What she needed was some space to think. The very idea that she was being watched creeped her out in a way that being followed by her father's private hire when she'd first started dating Rafe didn't. This was different. She turned the car off just as Kerry's front door opened, and she stepped out.

Kerry walked to the car. Avery got out.

"Hey, girl." She opened her back door, pulled out her suitcase and came around to the sidewalk, where Kerry was standing. They hugged.

"You good?" Kerry asked, the concern etched between her brows.

"Yeah," she said on a breath. "Thanks for letting me stay here."

"Girl, please. Come on in." She draped her arm over Avery's shoulders and they walked inside.

"Can I get you anything?" Kerry asked once they were settled inside.

"No. Thanks. Just want to sit here for a minute."

Kerry plopped down in the side chair opposite Avery, just as her cellphone rang. Avery took the phone from her back pocket. "It's Rafe," she mouthed to Kerry, who eased out of her chair and walked away.

Avery dragged in a breath and pressed the talk icon. "Hey."

"Avery, what's going on? I got a call from

Alice. She said you packed your bag and went to Kerry's."

"I got here a little while ago."

"Why!"

"I went for a run this morning. When I was on my way back to the house, I was stopped by a reporter who wanted to know had I moved in. He wanted me to comment on our engagement." She heard his muffled expletives. "I can't be a target, Rafe. Especially now when I'm getting ready to go back to work."

"I know," he ground out. "I get it. Look, I'll take care of it."

"I really don't see what you can do. This is the media. You know better than anyone they can be relentless, and if one of them is following me, there will be others."

"Every media storm has its moment. This is going to disappear the minute something more interesting happens." He paused. "Darlin' . . . I'm sorry. I don't want any of this for you."

"I know that. It's not your fault. But I have to do this for now. I need you to understand that."

"I don't like it, but I get it. My only concern is you."

She sighed softly. "How is everything back home?"

71

"So far . . . okay. I'll see the family tomorrow. You'll see the doctor on Monday, right?"

"Yes. I don't have a choice if I want to go back to work." She would do whatever she needed to do to get cleared. Even if it meant lying about what she was still going through.

"And the headaches?"

Avery closed her eyes and as if conjuring a spell the lie slipped over her lips. "I'm fine."

"You *would* tell me, right?"

She hesitated a beat. "Of course."

Rafe blew out a breath. "I'll be back in about a week. Sooner if I can get everything tied up here. I need to fly up to New York, get with Quinten."

"Can't wait."

"We're gonna get through this, darlin' — walk down that aisle and into forever. Me and you."

Her heart always shook loose from its anchor when he talked like that . . . about them, forever. She smiled. " 'Kay."

"Talk to you tomorrow."

"Absolutely."

"I love you, Avery. No matter what."

"Love you, too. Bye." She disconnected the phone and wondered what he meant by "no matter what" again?

■ ■ ■ ■

He had to get away from his thoughts at least for a little while. He went down to the garage and fired up his Harley. Not long after, he was racing along the blacktop with the thick Louisiana air whizzing around him.

The early Saturday-evening traffic was relatively light, allowing him to hopscotch across the three lanes at will. Beyond the ribbons of white and yellow lines, rooftops and spires, the sun took its final bow, stretching its fingers of orange and gold across the horizon in a last-ditch effort to cling to its illuminating power. Sunset always had a calming effect on him. As a kid, whenever he'd gotten into trouble at school or was feeling misunderstood, his mother, Louisa, would take him out on the back porch and they would watch the sun set over the lake that ran behind their home. His mother would remind him that the end of the day was the time to put all the happenings of the day to rest. It was the time to think about tomorrow and how to do things better or different. Funny he should think about that now.

Rafe bore down on the accelerator the

moment there was an opening. He flipped down his tinted visor against the glare, leaned into the bike until they were one unit of flesh, bone and metal. Together they rode into the wind that pushed against him, tried to hold him back. This was what he did, who he was, even as the counsel of his mother still flowed through his veins. He pushed through the obstacles that tried to hold him back, whether it was his controlling father, who wanted to mold him into his image, a relentless media that chronicled his life and made up the rest, or the laundry list of wannabe matchmakers and conniving women that wanted nothing more than to claim the Lawson name. It was true that a bunch of what was in his way was a result of his own creation. He laughingly told his siblings that he had a "rebel gene" that compelled him to buck the status quo at every turn.

But in a few months he would be a husband, and if he wanted his marriage to last, he was going to have to permanently shake off the tentacles of his past and find a way to quiet, if not silence, the rebel in his soul.

CHAPTER 9

Avery couldn't seem to shake Rafe's cryptic comment when they last spoke. If there was one thing that she'd learned about him in the time they'd been together, it was that Rafe Lawson was *never* vague. He said exactly what he meant, and the world be damned. It was one of the many qualities that she loved about him. His honesty and exactness made her feel secure, knowing that whatever he said, whatever commitment he made, it was for real. This was the first time she didn't feel that way.

She stuck her feet in her flip-flop slippers. Kerry was on duty, doing a double. She had the house to herself until at least nine, and the emptiness of the two-bedroom condo echoed the sentiments of her stomach as she walked down the hallway to the kitchen. She passed the rows of framed black-and-white photos that hung singularly and in groups, telling the story of Kerry's growing-up years with her two older brothers and sister, the vacations, holiday gatherings, her handsome exes. She stopped in front of one photo that captured the image of Kerry at her college graduation, flanked by her parents, who gazed at their daughter with unabashed love and pride.

The image of her own college graduation day took its place in front of her eyes. She saw herself, unsmiling with her father standing next to her, his stiff arm draped ceremoniously across her shoulder. She realized with a pang just how different she was from her best and only friend, how her life and family were so very different from Kerry's. Different from Rafe's. She longed for what they had and at the same time was terrified of it. She stroked the outline of Kerry's photographed face. When you had *all that,* there was more to lose. She could take the singular loses. She was expert at that. But the love of a family . . .

A searing razor-edged pain sliced through her skull, bringing her to her knees. She reached out to break her fall but took several of the photos crashing to the floor with her. Hot tears sprang from her eyes, clouding her already hazy vision. Her stomach roiled from the pain. Down on her hands and knees she drew in long, deep breaths, until the pounding lessened and her vision began to clear. She drew her knees up to her chest and leaned against the cool off-white wall, and this time the tears weren't from the pain but from fear.

She lost track of how long she'd sat huddled against the wall. When the pain subsided enough for her to attempt to push herself to a standing position, the photo of Kerry and her family lay cracked at her feet. The metaphor didn't escape her, but her next problem was explaining what happened to Kerry.

Kerry wouldn't flip about the cracked glass of the framed picture, but rather what caused it. Her worry would be about her friend.

Slowly she picked up the photographs that had fallen and gingerly returned them to their rightful places on the wall, except the one she'd damaged. She took that one with her into the living room and set it on the table.

The pain in her head lessened to a dull throb and a steady beat behind her right eye. That was a good thing. She'd get through this episode. She put one foot in front of the other, returned to her room for her medication and crawled back into bed, where Kerry found her hours later curled in a fetal position.

"There you are," Jacqueline greeted as Rafe walked out to the back patio on Sunday afternoon. The family, extended and immediate, were in various stages of lying back. "Started to think you weren't coming."

"Wouldn't miss it, Aunt J." He kissed her cheek. "Jackson, good to see you, man. It's been a minute." He shook his brother-in-law's hand.

Jackson rose with the handshake and clapped Rafe heartily on the back. "Looking good, bruh. Life must be treating you lovely."

Rafe chuckled. "Can't complain." He beamed at his younger brother Justin. "Yo, bruh." The brothers embraced, clapped each other on the back.

"Hey, beautiful lady." He leaned down and kissed Bailey's cheek.

"Hey," she said with a smile, and squeezed Rafe's hand.

His sister Desiree was glued to the hip of her husband Spence, who had a protective arm around his very pregnant wife.

"You look like you're ready to pop any minute, sis." He squatted down next to her.

He playfully rested his ear against her belly. "Sounds like you have a football team in there, girl."

Desiree swatted his arm. "That's 'cause I'm hungry," she said over her laughter.

"Right," he teased. "Spence, long time, man. How are you?"

The two men shook hands.

"Can't complain. It's all good. How's Avery? Recovering okay?"

"She's doing well. Ready to go back to work."

"Glad to hear that. Give her my regards."

Rafe bobbed his head in agreement.

The back door swung open and Dominique stepped out with a platter of seasoned chicken for the grill. Her diamond-shaped face and long-lashed eyes lit up. "Rafe!" She set the platter down on the table and threw her arms around her brother. "So good to see you," she said against his chest and then looked up at him. "Glad you came. I have so much to tell you. Is Avery coming? Is she here?"

"Good to see you, too, sis," he said. "And no, Avery's not coming. She's in Virginia. Goes back to work tomorrow."

Rafe worked on keeping his expression impassive but was pretty sure he'd failed when he saw Dominique's bright smile dim.

She knew him well. "We need to talk," he said low enough so only she could hear.

Dominique pursed her polished lips. "Sure." She sauntered over to the table where she'd deposited the tray of chicken and walked with it over to the grill.

Jacqueline shot Rafe a warning side-eye, to which he responded in kind and smoothly moved out of her line of fire. His aunt Jacquie was definitely not one to play with, but she also hated scenes. She wouldn't intentionally do anything to publicly put him or his sister on blast.

He moved toward Raymond, who was refilling the cooler with bottles of beer.

"I'll take a cold one," he said, coming up behind Raymond.

"You got it." He pulled a bottle from the bottom of the cooler.

Moisture ran down the sides of the bottle and made the golden contents shimmer in the afternoon sun.

"Thanks, man. How's it going?" He grabbed an opener and popped off the cap.

"Taking it easy today. Actually, I head out next week on an assignment. Trying to spend 'quality' time with my wife before I go," he said with a toss of his head in Jacqueline's direction.

"Where to this time?"

"Afghanistan. Getting imbedded with the army. Three weeks."

"I don't know what I'm supposed to do for three weeks," Jacqueline said, before slipping her arm around her husband's waist.

Raymond chuckled, leaned down and kissed her forehead. "Woman, when have you ever not had something to keep you busy, and we have Paris to look forward to when I'm done."

"Yes," she cooed and turned fully into his embrace.

Rafe gripped the beer bottle tighter. Paris had been a city that he'd loved, visited many times for business and pleasure, but after the bombing and almost losing Avery and his father, Paris would never be the same. He tossed his head back and took a long, deep swallow of the icy brew and then followed the path to the grill.

"You plan to help or stand around looking cute?" Dominique teased while she continued to place the seasoned wings on the grill.

"So you *do* think I'm cute?" he tossed back and came to stand next to her.

"Hmm." She looked him up and down. "You'll do. Hand me the sauce in that bowl, please."

Rafe retrieved the bowl and started brushing the wings with sauce. "We have a problem, sis."

"I figured as much." She turned to him with her hand planted on her hip. "What?"

"The wedding. Avery feels like you and Desi and Lee Ann are making it more ya'll's than hers."

Dominique's neck jerked back. "What? Why?"

He gave her his you-know-damn-well-why look.

She pursed her lips and huffed. "I just want your wedding to be everything, Rafe." She pressed her palm against his chest and fluttered her lashes.

Rafe refused to give in and held back a smile. "Don't try to work me, D."

"Me? Work you?" She closed the cover to the grill and then turned back to her brother. "None of us want to take over the wedding. And we certainly don't want Avery to feel that she's not a part of the planning. I guess we . . . *I* got carried away. This is a big deal. You? Married?" She flashed him her dimpled smile. "We never thought it would happen . . . after Janae," she said softly.

His jaw clenched. *Janae*. "It is kinda crazy." He pushed out a breath and shoved his hands into his pants' pockets. "But it's a little more complicated than just wedding planning on steroids."

"What else?"

"I know you were in your zone when you made the announcement to the papers . . ." He explained Avery's reaction, right up to her being accosted on the street by a reporter.

"Damn," she whispered. "I had no idea."

"Yeah. Me either. For us the media is like a regular Tuesday, but not Avery. And she has concerns that it could affect her job."

"I never thought of that." She looked up at him with wide eyes. "I am so sorry, Rafe. I swear. I'll fix it," she added quickly, and Rafe could see the wheels turning in her head.

"Slow down. I don't want you doing anything else. Got it?" he said with a warning glare. "We'll keep a low profile, and hopefully they'll latch onto something more interesting."

Dominique folded her arms. "Fine."

More than any of his other siblings, he and Dominique were the closest, even more so than Dom and her twin sister. Like his aunt Jacqueline said, they were kindred spirits. She was the one who would nurse his wounds after one of his fights or tumbles from his motorcycle and took his side even when she kinda thought he was wrong. They shared hurts and secrets, and other than Quinten, she was the only one who came close to understanding how losing Janae totally changed his DNA.

He kissed the top of her head the way he did when she was a teenager and would get busted sneaking in late, and she'd cry on his chest about how her latest punishment was going to ruin her life. But they weren't kids anymore. This was the real deal. Dom had to realize that her actions had consequences. Like him, she was driven by raw emotion. He released her, and when she looked up at him, he knew they'd make it all work; they always did.

"Promise me that you'll let me handle it," Rafe said.

Dominique pursed her polished lips. "Fine. But I'm here when you need me."

"I know that." He draped his arm around her shoulder and pushed out a breath. "Enough of all this. What I really want to know is, where's your etouffe? You know I can't come home and not get my favorite."

Dominique giggled, and for the moment all was right at the Lawson house.

"How are you feeling today?" Kerry asked.

She lifted her mug of mint tea and brought it to her lips.

"I'm fine. No after-effects." She lathered her everything bagel with a dollop of cream cheese.

Kerry put down her mug and rested her forearms on the wood tabletop. "Avery . . . I know you want to power through this, but I saw you yesterday."

Avery glanced up from beneath her lashes and then quickly focused on her bagel. "I'm fine."

"You're not fine, A! What if you're on duty and you have an episode? Are you willing to risk the safety of your assignment and yourself for a point of pride?"

Avery lifted her chin. "As long as the doctor clears me, I'll come back. If not . . . I'll have to follow his instructions."

Kerry studied her friend, heaved a sigh. She held up her hand. "Fine." She pushed back from the table. "Want to ride in together, or are you taking your car?"

"I'll take my car. No telling how today will turn out."

"Look, even if you're not approved for full duty, at least you'll be back in the office, even if it is desk duty."

Inwardly Avery cringed. They may as well take her badge and gun if she was going to ride the desk. That was not what she trained and worked so hard for. Whatever she needed to do to ensure that she was fully back on the job, she would do. The problem was she wasn't sure who would be harder to convince, the doctor or Kerry.

"I'll cross that bridge when we get there." She wiped her mouth with a paper napkin and put her plate in the sink.

"Do you want me to go with you? Moral support? I can call and let them know I'll be late."

"No. Not necessary. I'll be fine. Ready?"

Being back at the Agency was the shot of adrenaline she needed. For the first time in months, she felt energized. Walking through the doors, seeing the familiar signposts of plaques and portraits, she knew she was home again. This was where she belonged, what she'd worked for, deserved to be.

"Agent Richards, welcome back," the security guard at the check-in station greeted. "Great work in Paris," he added.

"Good to be back. Thanks." She swiped her ID, placed her weapon and badge in the plastic bin and walked through the metal detector.

She gathered her belongings on the other side and walked toward the elevator. The doors slid soundlessly open. Avery walked to the back of the elevator and pressed her back against the wall as other agents and staff boarded, floor by floor.

For days leading up to her exam she'd refrained from taking any medication. She needed to be able to show them that the meds were no longer necessary. The doctor gave her a full exam, took some blood and urine samples and asked her a laundry list of questions, from her eating to sleeping habits. He'd focused for quite some time on the headaches and how she'd been able to wean herself off the medication.

She'd practiced long and hard on the lie that she would tell, and looked him right in the eye when she told him with a straight face that she'd been pain-free for weeks — episodes over.

He'd nodded as he listened and took notes. Finally, he looked up and smiled. "As long as the tests come back with no problems, I can give you medical clearance. They should be in by the end of the week. In the meantime, I'll call over to headquarters and let the director know that you can be returned to limited duty until the tests come in." He'd stood. "Welcome back."

She'd breathed a major sigh of relief, shook the doctor's hand and walked out, confident that she'd gotten a part of her life back.

The elevator doors opened on her floor. Her heart suddenly began to race. Her right temple throbbed. She sucked in a lungful of air, put one foot in front of the other and walked off. She would get through this. She had to. She plastered a smile on her face as the pain intensified.

"Good morning, Agent Richards. Welcome back. You can go right in. The director is expecting you."

"Thank you." She straightened her shoulders and walked toward the director's office. She knocked on the closed door.

"Come in."

Avery stepped inside. Director Fischer stood when she entered. "Agent Richards. Come in. Come in. Have a seat."

"Thank you, sir." She focused on sitting in the chair and not the pounding behind her left eye. She linked her fingers together on her lap.

"So . . . how are you?"

"Good. Feeling great. I'm confident that the doctor will give me a clean bill of health."

"He's already called. His preliminary report will be here in the morning, but from what he told me, you're cleared for limited duty."

"Thank you, sir."

"You do understand that limited means no fieldwork for now."

"Yes, sir. I understand."

"Good." He slapped his palm on his desk for emphasis and stood. He extended his hand, which she reached in and shook.

"I'll get back to work," she said with a smile.

"Yes, and set up with my assistant your firing-range review and field physical."

"Of course."

"And . . . as you know your name is still in the running for the assistant deputy director position. We put everything on hold while you were recovering. Of course, going forward, much of the evaluation will hinge on the final medical report and your field physical."

"Yes, sir. Of course. I understand."

Director Fischer gave a short nod. "Welcome back."

"Thank you, sir." She turned to leave, forcing herself to put one foot in front of the other. The top of her head felt as if it would explode. She needed her medication and she needed it now before she passed out. "I'll call to make the appointments," she managed to say to the director's assistant and then hurried down the hall to the elevator.

She smiled and waved, made brief cursory small talk to the colleagues that greeted her en route to her office. Once inside, she quickly locked the door. Her vision began to blur. She breathed in deeply through her nose while fumbling in her purse for her pain medication. Her hands shook as she tried to twist the childproof cap off. She shoved two tablets into her mouth and swallowed them dry.

Still leaning with her back against the door, she shut her eyes and imagined the calming waters of the Caribbean ebbing and flowing toward white, sandy shores. She saw herself drifting away toward the horizon, carried along by the soothing blue waters.

By degrees the intensity of the pain lessened. She squinted against the light coming in from the window behind her desk and slowly crossed the room. No sooner had she sat down, her desk phone rang.

She reached for the phone and slowly brought it to her ear. "Richards."

"Hey, girl. Didn't want to call your cell in case you were still in the middle of things. How'd it go with the doc and Fischer?"

"Perfect." She gave Kerry a quick run-down.

"Whew. That's a relief. Well, I know you need to get settled and up to speed. I'll see you later at the house. I have off-site work today."

"Okay. See you later."

Avery hung up the phone, leaned back against the headrest of her chair. The pain meds were starting to kick in. It worked. She should be happy. This was what she wanted. But at what cost? Her eyes filled. At what cost?

Chapter 10

Rafe checked in his desk drawer for the keys to his silver Lexus. It had been a while since he'd taken his birthday present to himself out on the road. Although the car was more than a year old, it barely had eight thousand miles on it and still had that brand-new leather smell. He'd treated himself to the luxury automobile to celebrate the success of his foundation landing a major grant and, of course, his thirty-fifth birthday. Cars, clothes, travel, money were abundances that were commonplace in his life. He didn't grow up worrying about his next meal or if he'd get ragged at school for not having the latest Jordans. The Lawsons traveled in the rarified air that most black folk only dreamed about. But "all that stuff" never meant much to him. It was just the way things were. But as he traveled across the country, he came to understand the adage, "to whom much is given, much is expected."

It took him a minute to find his way, but he did when he launched his foundation. They were making real progress, and this year would be the first that the foundation would be able to award three full college scholarships for musicians of color. His father did it his way through politics, and Rafe would make his mark with music.

He grabbed his black, hip-length leather jacket from the hook by the door and walked out to the garage through the kitchen.

For all the cities he'd visited there was always something special about his hometown of New Orleans that drew him back. The rich, dark history and culture of the city of New Orleans exuded an energy that went beyond the parties in the streets, sticky pralines, spicy gumbo, Anne Rice's vampire novels, Mardi Gras, impromptu street performances and iconic structures. It was the people that made it magical — with their big hearty smiles and the swag in their step within their multi-colored milieu, even in the midst of despair and abject poverty. The city, like blood, flowed through his veins, and each time he returned home, he was transfused.

Behind the wheel, the thought of permanently moving away gathered speed in concert with the Lexus. It was a bridge that he and Avery would have to cross. But as he drove through the streets that ranged from palatial estates tucked behind professionally manicured gardens and wrought-iron gates to the trailers and prefab homes occupied by the survivors of Katrina, to the lull of the mighty Mississippi, he was no longer sure that he'd be willing to give it up.

He exited the I-610 and took the main streets into downtown. His office was located on Canal Street, once the pathway for horse-drawn carriages for the wealthy, while others rode the streetcars that withstood the test of time and the upriver boundary of the French Quarter. Street parking was at a premium along this stretch that was peppered with luxury hotels like the Ritz Carlton or the Astor Crowne Plaza, which were converted from their historic predecessors, the high-end stores — Maison Blanche, Godchaux's and D.H. Holmes — and theaters and restaurants that overflowed with residents and tourists at all hours of the day and night.

Rafe drove past his office and the Joy Theater, went around the block to the lot. He maintained a monthly account for days like this. Walking back to the building where his office was housed, he was pleasantly assaulted by the live music floating from the opened doorways of restaurants, followed by low- and high-pitched laughter and the unmistakable 'Nawlins twang.

Tourists strolled wide-eyed, laden with bags, and in awe of the assault on the senses from every direction, while the residents reveled in the ordinary everyday-ness of their lives.

Rafe pulled on the vertical silver bar handle of the glass door and stepped into the refreshingly chilly air, a respite from the wooly weight of humidity, a hallmark of Louisiana weather.

He took the elevator up to the tenth floor, which housed the suite of six offices and a conference room. For now the space was large enough to accommodate the needs of the RBL Foundation, but Rafe knew that, as his vision continued to expand, so would the need for more space.

"Halle, how are you?" he greeted his receptionist, before he plucked a rose from the vase that held the dozen he'd sent her like clockwork each week. He handed it to her with a bow.

Halle's laughter, which always sounded like runs on a Steinway piano, filled the reception space with her everready joy.

"Why, Mr. Lawson," she purred, lowering

her long lashes over rum-colored eyes and slowly dragging the bud of the rose beneath her nose, "how gallant of you, kind sir."

Rafe grinned. "I can only try. What do I need to know?"

Halle easily shifted back to full business mode. "The board members should be here in about an hour. I've ordered lunch from Creole House, and Danielle said she wanted to see you as soon as you arrived."

"Thanks. Danielle's in her office?"

"Yes." He started off but then stopped and turned back. He pointed a warning finger in her direction. "Tell whoever it is that keeps sending you flowers that I'm a very jealous boss," he teased with a wicked glint in his eyes.

She shook her head and laughed at their inside joke. "Will do."

Rafe strode down the carpeted corridor, passing the five office spaces that occupied the spine of the space. Along the soft white walls hung framed photos of the galas, the political and fund-raising events, and the staff and members of the board. He turned left at the end of the hall, away from the conference room, and stopped at Danielle's office, which was across the hall from his. He knocked on the closed door.

"Yes. Come in."

Notary name: WA8rIE 4?/A

Total checkouts: 3

3
Total checkouts for session:
12:04

Item price: $31.99
Date due: 4/18/2019,23:59
12:04
Date charged: 3/28/2019,
[large print]
Title: The masterpiece [large
print]
Item ID: 36...003722787
[large print]
Title: The secret of clouds

Item price: $30.99
Date due: 4/18/2019,23:59
12:04
Date charged: 3/28/2019,
[large print]
Title: A sister's survival

Item price: $31.99
Date due: 4/18/2019,23:59
12:04
Date charged: 3/28/2019,
[large print]
Title: When I'm w...

(828) 586-3334
Margaret E Heaga...

Rafe eased the door open and poked his head through the gap. "Busy? Halle said you needed to see me."

Danielle whipped off her designer glasses — today they were blue rimmed — and placed them on the desk, which was stacked on either side of her with folders. "Hey." She waved him inside. "Come on in."

Danielle had been with him from the beginning. They'd met through his sister Dominique's business, First Impression. Danielle had been instrumental in promoting Dominique's dream to the general public. But her skills extended beyond publicity. She had an MBA with a specialty in finance, was detail-oriented, great with seeing the small things in the big-picture world of Rafe Lawson, could run numbers in her head at lightning speed, knew what he needed before he needed it and, at the drop of a hat, she could stand in for him at any venue. When he took all that into account, he knew he was making the right decision and was confident that the board would agree.

She leaned back in her chair, rubbed the bridge of her short, slender nose. "How are you? It's been a minute." She tucked her shoulder-length, bone-straight hair behind her ears.

Rafe came around and sat in the over-stuffed paisley-print chair opposite her desk. He draped his right ankle across his left thigh. "I know." He blew out a breath. "Lot going on, but I knew I had you holding everything down. Anything I need to know before this meeting?"

She reached into her desk and pulled out a red folder and handed it to him. "Basic notes on where the scholarships stand, list of donors, quarterly projections and an outline for the summer fund-raiser."

Rafe flipped open the folder and quickly scanned the very detailed notes. He bobbed his head. "Thanks. Anything else?" He closed the folder and rested it on his thigh.

"The scholarships are a big deal, Rafe. Three full rides." She beamed in delight. "That was no small feat. So the roll out and the event have to be larger than life. I've already started the plan, secured the venue. I did want to sit down with your sister Desiree. With her being on the city council, it can only help to bring in more support with her connections."

"Not a problem. We want big-ticket donors at the event, along with the presidents of the universities."

"On my list."

"I want to personally sign all of the invitations."

She nodded and made a note. "I've asked Halle to put together a list of caterers."

"No. I'll get my brother-in-law Spence to handle the menu. His staff is big enough to handle it."

"Got it." Danielle tipped her head to the side, her dark chocolate eyes locking on Rafe. She put her notes aside. "How are you . . . really? And how is Avery? I've seen the papers lately."

Rafe's brows rose and fell. He pushed out a breath and brought Danielle up to speed.

She linked her slender fingers together, and Rafe wondered as he spoke how she was able to be so productive with her long embellished nails.

"If there's anything I can do, you know you only have to say the word," she said once he was done.

" 'Preciate that." He pushed to his feet. "See you at the meeting."

"Yep."

He left and went to his office across the hall.

As much as he would like to take total credit for the foundation and its mission, the idea was originally Janae's. She planted the seed of the idea years earlier, when they were on a weekend getaway to Aruba as part of her social-work studies. They visited several schools on the island. After talking with many of the students, they were both moved by the students' love of learning and desire to go to college one day. Unfortunately, that would not be a reality for many of them. Janae said that, back home, so many students were faced with the same fate, and with the Lawson family name, connections and wealth, they could make a difference — offer scholarships to deserving students. He let the idea sit, not sure if he was really the one to take on that role.

Still, it wasn't until years after he lost her, after no longer caring about much of anything, that her vision took root again. He knew that if he was ever going to find his way back to some sense of normal, he needed to find a purpose in his life that went beyond satisfying his own needs. With the legal help of his brother Justin, he formed the foundation. He sat behind his desk and looked around at the plaques and framed citations on the wall. He shook his head and smiled in bemusement. Had someone told him ten years ago that this was where he would be, he would have laughed in his face. Now, he couldn't see otherwise.

He leaned back and exhaled as a melancholy smile shadowed his mouth. Janae would be proud. Her spirit was part of the success of the foundation. Whenever he spent time here, he often wondered what things would be like if Janae was with him. His smile widened, sure that Janae's "save the world" mantra would be imprinted on all their endeavors. That's why it was going to be hard to let the board know that he was turning the reins over to Danielle so that he could take a back seat. The notion that he would possibly have to relocate to DC was already difficult, but if he could set things up so that the transition would be smooth, that's what he would do.

He frowned, stroked his smooth chin. Funny, if Janae was here, this would not be on the table. Reflexively his jaw tightened. But she wasn't. He pushed back from the desk, pulled the lower drawer open and pulled out a striped tie — part of boardroom décor, which he always bucked against. But wearing a tie on today of all days was the least he could do.

Rafe took his suit jacket from the hook and slipped it on. Hopefully Danielle would take the announcement well, since he'd chosen to hold his cards close to his chest until this meeting. Harder for her to say no.

■ ■ ■ ■

"You blindsided me," Danielle said, staring across at Rafe. Her palms were planted on her desk, her body tense. "Why? And why the hell didn't you say something?" She held up her hand. "No. Don't bother. I know why you did it . . . so that I wouldn't say no."

Rafe's attempts to look sheepish didn't move Danielle.

"There's that," he admitted and slid his hands into his pockets. "Look, there's no one more qualified to run the foundation." He slowly paced in front of her desk, his head lowered in thought as he spoke. "You do it anyway." He turned to face her. "You deserve the title of CEO and the perks that go along with it. I'll still have my hand in — you know that. But you'll officially run the day-to-day."

Danielle looked directly at him. "I don't know what to say." She paused. "Thank you for the confidence you have in me. I won't let you down."

"I know that." He gave her that half grin. "So . . . we good?"

"Did you give me a choice? Yes," she said with a conceding smile, "we're good."

He loosened his tie, pulled it from around his neck and then stuck it in his pants pocket. "Let me know when the invites are ready for my signature, and have Halle draft up a press release with the announcement." He winked. "Talk to you soon."

His next stop was his club on Bourbon Street, centered in the heart of the French Quarter, renowned since the mid-1800s as the hot spot for Mardi Gras. He could have chosen any number of locations for a night-spot in New Orleans, but the energy, the history, the thrill of the Quarter was visceral. There was no place like it in the world. Although his club was one of many, what he offered was a menu prepared by a chef who trained under Emeril himself. Pair that with his highly skilled bartender who created a one-of-a-kind version of the infamous Hurricane for weekend guests, and Lawsons was *the* place to be. It didn't hurt that he often played a set and used his connections in the music industry to bring in some of the top-named jazz musicians.

His co-managers, Marcus and his wife, Antoinette, ran Lawsons like a well-oiled machine. The staff was happy, the customers were thrilled and business boomed.

When he popped into the club the lunch crowd had dwindled down to those who struggled with the reality that they had to return to work. His club was fashioned after the clubs he'd visited in Europe; although large in space, they were designed with a feeling of intimacy. Circular tables that seated no more than four and private banquettes for larger parties were situated on gradient levels. The dark wood walls were adorned with signed black-and-white photographs of film, television, athletic and musical stars. Every seat in the house had perfect views of the stage, and the dim, recessed lighting provided the perfect ambiance.

"Mr. Lawson!" Antoinette walked toward him from the back while wiping her hands on a towel. "I didn't expect you. Everything okay?"

Rafe leaned down and buzzed her cheek, lightly squeezed her shoulder. "In town for a few days."

"Congratulations on your engagement."

"Thank you." He took a quick look around. "How's everything going?"

"Busy," she said on a breath and with a full-bodied smile. "We had to hire two more wait staff."

"Whatever you need to do. Who's on the entertainment lineup?"

"Thinking about sitting in?"

Rafe chuckled. "Never know." He folded

his arms and leaned against the bar.

She gave him a rundown on the upcoming performers.

"Real tempting," he said, nodding his head in appreciation. "Probably on my next visit. Tryin' to get Quinten Parker to come down."

"Now, that would be fantastic."

"Flying up to New York in the morning. Gonna twist his arm."

"Make sure you do. Me and Marcus will make it *the* event."

"I know ya'll will. Anyway, I'm out. Just wanted to stop in and see how things were going. I'll be back in town in a few weeks. But anything come up before then, you know you can always reach me."

"Marcus will be sorry he missed you," Antoinette said while they walked toward the front door.

"We'll catch up next time. Let him know the new website for the club is fire! The shots of the interior, menu, photos of the performers — perfect. Brotha got skills."

Antoinette laughed. "All those classes he took are finally paying off."

"For sure." He pulled the front door open. "Thank you for all your hard work. Lawsons is a success because of you and Marcus, and I appreciate ya'll."

"That means a lot."

"I'm only a phone call away. Whatever you need." He wagged a finger. "And I'm gonna get Quinten down here."

"I know you will," she said with a smile. "Safe travels."

"Thanks." He stepped out into the late afternoon and was embraced by the meaty arms of heat. He muttered a useless curse under his breath and walked to his car. If he was going to have to pull up stakes and relocate to DC, at least he knew that his enterprises were in capable hands.

CHAPTER 11

"I'm going back to my place after work," Avery said as she and Kerry walked into a staff meeting.

"Are you sure? You know you can stay as long as you want."

They found two seats in the back of the room, which was already filled with about thirty agents by the time they arrived. The agents would always joke that if all of them were in one room, who was guarding the hen house?

"Thanks. I appreciate it, but I think the dust has finally settled. Like Rafe said, the reporters will find something else to write about." She shrugged. "I guess they did. And it's time for me to put all the pieces of my life back in place, and going home is one of them."

"Okay. But you have a key if you change your mind."

" 'Preciate that."

"Say no more. Do you, sis."

The director took to the podium and went through his mind-numbing update. Fisher had about as much warmth and personality as an empty plastic bag, but he was good at his job. He was not a nurturer like his predecessor. He didn't groom his agents; he simply expected them to rise to the challenge.

Avery let her mind wander while Director Fisher spoke. She'd been back at work for almost two weeks. She'd passed her field test and her labs were clean. Today was her first day back on detail — late luncheon gathering for the senators and donors at the Watergate Hotel. She was assigned to Senator Kevin Banks, a Republican, but she wouldn't hold that against him. Briefly she glanced around the room, taking in her colleagues. They were all nondescript. They could be anybody or no one, and she fit right in with her well-fitted dark blue suit, hair pulled back into a tight knot at the nape of her neck, dark shades at the ready and underarm holster hugging her agency-issued Glock. She was a part of something bigger than herself, but without the emotional commitment. Maybe that was why this line of work suited her in ways that relationships didn't. If one of her colleagues were . . . lost, there would be one nearly identical to replace that person. That wasn't true of relationships when feelings and desires were involved. Here you weren't allowed the luxury of "feeling" anything. You did your job.

She shifted in her seat, crossed her legs. Things were finally returning to a life that she understood, where she was in control. She only took the pain meds when the pain became unbearable, and no one was the wiser. She got her job back, and she was determined to get the promotion that she deserved.

"Not as boring as usual," Kerry whispered as everyone began to file out.

Avery blinked away her musings, smiled and stood. "Thank goodness." She checked her watch. "I'm on duty in thirty minutes. What's on your agenda?"

"I'm stationed at the Capitol. Easy day for me."

"I'll give you a call later." She patted Kerry's shoulder and headed off in the opposite direction.

The standard black Chevy Suburban was parked in front of Senator Banks's townhouse in Reston, Virginia. Avery and her partner for the evening, Agent Brian Halstead, were stationed and waiting.

"Good to see you back on duty, Richards," Halstead said.

"Feels good to be back." She scanned the area and adjusted her headset.

"I hear you're in the running for a promotion."

Senator Banks's front door opened. Avery and Brian moved in unison toward the front door and then escorted Senator Banks and his wife into the vehicle. Senator Banks was the chair of the Foreign Relations Committee and a ranking member of the Judiciary Committee.

"In the meantime," she said, taking a last look around before swinging into the front passenger seat, "I still have my job to do."

She slid open the partition that separated the security team from the passengers. "ETA is twenty-five minutes, sir."

"Thank you."

Avery shut the partition and focused on the road and the afternoon ahead. Tonight she would sleep in her own bed, move one more step toward normalcy.

Agents were accustomed to the press hovering, jockeying for position to get a shot or shout out a question. They took it in stride, remaining focused on their assignment and protecting those under their care.

When Avery exited the car to quickly check the scene around the entrance to the hotel, nothing could have stunned her more than to hear her name shouted out from the clutch of reporters huddled nearby.

Her heart rate escalated so quickly that her breath caught in her throat. Instinctively her head swung toward the sound.

Senator Banks and his wife stopped in mid-step.

"When is the wedding, Agent Richards?"

"Has Rafe Lawson stopped his playboy ways?"

"Are you still going to work after the wedding?"

"Does Senator Richards approve?"

Oh, my God. Her stomach seesawed.

Brian Halstead threw her a look of alarm and quickly guided the senator and his wife inside. Avery drew in a breath and followed the group inside.

"What the hell was that?" Senator Banks demanded the instant they crossed the threshold.

"Senator . . . I apologize. Everything is under control."

He frowned. "It doesn't appear so, Agent Richards." He turned to Agent Halstead and spoke to him in hushed tones.

Halstead nodded. "Yes, sir." He turned to

Avery, and said in an undertone, "The senator wants you to wait here to be replaced by a backup agent. I'm sorry, Avery. I gotta make the call to headquarters."

Numbly she nodded, knowing that it was protocol if an agent was compromised. She felt sick. A million thoughts raced through her head. How could this be happening?

"I'm going inside with the senator and his wife. Backup will be here in ten. You'll take his car back to Central," Halstead said, returning to Avery after his call.

Avery swallowed. "Of course."

Agent Halstead turned and walked away.

Avery felt as if she was standing outside of her body. The feeling was surreal. She paced the lobby floor, and like clockwork her replacement arrived in exactly ten minutes. Her day only grew worse when she saw that Mike was her replacement.

"Director wants to see you when you get back."

"I'm sure," she managed to say.

Mike handed her the keys to the Suburban he'd driven to the Watergate.

She clenched her teeth to keep from screaming, gripped the keys in her hand, turned and walked outside, hoping that she wouldn't lay eyes on the reporter and be tempted to run him over.

CHAPTER 12

"Hey, Aunt J. Everything all right?"

"I . . . don't know how to say this."

Rafe opened the car door. "What is it?"

"I got a call a little while ago. On the house phone . . . the woman said she was Janae."

The air stopped in his chest. "What?" He gripped the side of the car door.

"That's what she said. She said she was Janae and she was trying to reach you."

Every muscle tensed. "No. That's not possible." He tried to move but couldn't. "Janae is dead, Aunt J. Dead."

"Sweetheart, I know. We all know, but she told me things that only Janae would have knowledge of."

The pulse in his right temple began to pound. He shook his head in denial. "What could some imposter possibly have to say to make you think it was Janae?" he snapped. Pure adrenaline pumped through him, send-

113

ing fire through his veins.

"She told me about the family photo that we took the summer before . . . everything happened in New York . . . and how she didn't feel right getting in the picture, and that you and Dominique insisted. How would this woman know that, Rafe?"

His thoughts swung back to that summer day. A family reunion cookout. Everyone was there — all his siblings, significant others of the time, his father, cousins, uncles, and his grandfather Clive presided over the festivities. Melanie Harte, the diva of soirees and matchmaking, was in charge of organizing the family shindig, from sending out the invites to the decorations, to the never-ending menu. He remembered how reluctant Janae was to join in the family photo and how Dominique told her that she was the closest thing to permanent that had ever come into Rafe's life and she "betta" get in that photo and act like it.

There was no way that some stranger would know that specific detail.

"Rafe, are you there?"

He blinked the past away. "Yes," he said in a bare whisper.

"Sweetie, what do you want to do? She left a number. It's a Florida area code."

The knot in his gut tightened. "Florida."

He'd never met her parents, who lived in Chicago, while they dated. "She always told me her parents wanted to relocate to Florida," he said, in a faraway tone of disbelief. He heard his aunt's sharp intake of breath.

"Rafe . . . could it be . . . after all this time?"

"I don't know how. But if what she says is true, why turn up now?"

"She said she saw the announcement of your engagement on one of the entertainment channels and knew she needed to reach you."

Rafe squeezed his eyes shut. His jaw tightened. He muttered a string of expletives. "Text the number to me."

"All right. And Rafe . . ."

"Yeah . . ."

"This isn't Dominique's fault. And whoever this woman is, if in fact she is Janae, you need to find out for certain."

Rafe blew out a breath. "Send me the text when you get a minute, Aunt J."

"I will." She paused. "Listen to me . . . be easy, Rafe," she gently warned. "I know you . . ."

"I'm fine." He disconnected the call, pulled the door fully open and slid in behind the wheel.

His head was all over the place. He

couldn't get his thoughts to slow down long enough for them to make sense. How was this possible? He gripped the wheel. Janae Harper was dead. She was one of the countless souls lost that day in the World Trade Center disaster. True, her remains were never discovered, but no one, her family included, believed that she was alive. He'd spent the next two years after the tragedy doing all that he could to find some sign of her, all to no avail. Over time he'd shoved his feelings way down inside and tried to move on.

For the most part he did keep his feelings and those memories at bay, but there were still those moments when he was alone, or heard a song, or caught a whiff of the perfume Janae used to wear that he'd stumble backward to that horrid day, and all that terror and soul-wrenching heartache would implode.

His phone chirped. The text was from his aunt, with Janae's number.

Rafe stared at the number until the image began to blur. Janae's face floated across the windshield. His temple throbbed.

He put the car in gear and somehow made it to his family home without getting into an accident. Shaken, he entered his home like a stranger. Nothing looked familiar. He blinked, shut the door behind him and walked inside. He went into his father's study.

Alive. He wouldn't believe it until he heard her voice for himself. He squeezed the cell phone in his palm. He walked over to the bar and poured a tumbler of bourbon, downed the liquid in two long swallows and poured another. He moved over to the easy chair and flopped down. The 407 area code of Florida burned behind his closed lids.

The bourbon was making fuzz around the sharp edges. But he needed a clear head. A clear head, 'cause this mess didn't make sense. It didn't. This was some b.s. — had to be. He pushed up from the couch, paced, thirsted for another drink but stopped himself.

Instead, he scrolled through his messages and stopped on the one from his aunt Jacqueline. He ran his tongue along his bottom lip, pressed his thumb on the number on the face of the phone. The call connected.

Each ring sent a shockwave through his system, but nothing could have prepared him for the sound of the voice on the other end.

"Hello?" the familiar voice said into the phone, piercing through his fog.

Rafe cleared his throat. "I was given this number —"

"Rafe! You called."

The knot in his gut hardened, expanded until it filled his chest. "Janae." The name stumbled across his lips.

"I wasn't sure you'd call, that you'd believe it was really me."

The voice was the same, the soft Southern lilt still there. "I'm still not sure . . . after all this time." His voice rose. "How? We — everyone believed you were killed in the towers. All this time," he repeated in disbelief. "You were alive all this time and you —"

"Please, I know this is hard, but let me explain."

"Explain! You let me believe you were dead. How do you explain that?"

"It's complicated. My injuries . . . were severe."

He felt as much as he heard the hitch of pain in her voice, and his anger instantly tempered. Slowly he sat down. This wasn't about him.

"There's still a lot I don't remember about that day. They told me when they pulled me out that I'd been buried under a lot of rubble. Broken bones, burns, dehydration . . . I was in a coma for over two months. When I finally woke up in the hospital I didn't remember anything, not even my own name."

Rafe felt sick. He struggled to imagine what she had endured. "But when you remembered . . . your family . . . why didn't someone tell me that you were alive?"

"I didn't remember. I only knew what I was being told. Through a bunch of tests and calls they finally found my parents. I didn't recognize them. They *told* me they were my parents and I believed them. I stayed in the hospital for almost six months . . . surgeries, rehab. When I was stable and strong enough to leave they took me to Florida."

A knifelike pain twisted in his chest. He struggled to process what she was telling him, tried to connect the dots. She'd had no memory. Two people claiming to be her parents took her back to Florida. How could he be sure that this was Janae and not someone who'd been led to believe that she was? Yet deep in his soul he knew the truth. He knew her voice. Whatever else may have changed, that did not. He'd heard her voice in his dreams for more than a decade.

"When pieces of my memory began to come back, the only thing that was ever clear was you."

The jolt of her words hit like a punch in the gut.

"Not everything . . . at first. In the beginning it was only images. I'd see your face, your eyes, your smile. It was my only constant. Over time I remembered more, but never about any other part of my life except with you and me."

Rafe listened in numbed silence while Janae told him about things they'd said to each other, places they'd been. She told him about the first time she asked about the scar on his right shoulder and he told her it happened in a motorcycle accident. Whatever reservations he may have had dissolved with every passing moment. This was Janae.

"But you still haven't told me why you never let me know you were alive."

"My parents made all the decisions. I asked them about you. They told me that bringing you back into my life wouldn't be fair to you. That it was best if you thought I was dead." She uttered what sounded like a sad laugh. "When I looked at myself in the mirror, when I had to be helped out of bed, when the pain would be so bad on some nights that I wanted to die . . . I believed them. Why should I burden you?"

"God, Janae. If you know me like you say, you'd know better than to think that. We were in love. Young, but in love. You were my world. When I woke up in that hotel room and found you gone — then saw the towers come down." His voice broke. "A part of me died that day, too!" He slammed his fist against the wall. "Months and months and no word. I thought I'd go crazy. I blamed myself. If I hadn't taken you to New York —"

"Don't, please don't. You couldn't have known. No one could. How could either of us know that me taking a morning jog would change our world?" She paused. "I'm so sorry, Rafe."

He paced and ran a hand across his face, surprised that his eyes were damp. "Why now?" he asked quietly. "Why contact me now?"

"I never stopped loving you. Loving you kept me alive. I want to see you, Rafe."

"See me! Now you want to see me?"

"Rafe . . . please. At least think about it."

He swallowed over the burn in his throat. "I'll think about it."

"Thank you. I'll wait to hear from you. Goodbye, Rafe."

Rafe disconnected the call and squeezed the phone in his palm as if he could break it in half. His tense shoulders slumped.

"Hey, Rafe. I thought I heard someone

talking. What are you doing here?" Dominique asked, coming from the kitchen. He turned to face his sister. Alarm widened her eyes.

"What the hell?" She rushed over and grabbed his arm. "What's wrong?"

Rafe lowered his head a moment and then looked at his sister, debating whether he should tell her. "I . . . something's happened . . ."

"Oh my God, Rafe . . . but . . . I can't believe it. All this time. What the hell? Alive! How could she do this?" Her gaze of fury landed on her brother. Her tone immediately softened. "How are you though? I can't imagine what you're going through." She drew closer, looped her arms around his waist and rested her head on his chest. "I am so sorry."

"Nothing for you to be sorry about, sis. I'll deal with it."

She leaned back and looked up at him with astonishment widening her eyes. "Deal with it! How the hell do you deal with someone coming back from the freaking dead? This is some *Days of Our Lives* b.s."

If the situation wasn't so dire, he would laugh. Dominique was a true whiz at one-liners.

"Yeah, feels like a soap opera. Unreal."

Dominique dropped her arms and stepped back. "Have you told Avery?"

He shook his head slowly. "No. Not yet." He paused. "I'm going to Florida, first."

"Rafe . . ."

"I need to see her for myself."

The siblings stared into each other's eyes, understanding more than any words would convey.

Dominique nodded and gripped Rafe's upper arm. "You need me to fly shotgun, let me know. I'm there."

Rafe halfway grinned. "I'm good, sis. I can handle it. 'Preciate the offer."

Desiree waddled in from the downstairs bedroom. "What are ya'll gabbing about?" She yawned, looked from one to the other before lowering herself into the nearest seat.

Dominique flashed Rafe a questioning look. He gave a short nod.

"You're not planning to have my niece or nephew anytime soon?" Rafe quizzed, stalling for time.

Desiree looked up at him with her brows drawn together. "Huh?"

"Something you should know, but I don't want you getting yourself all worked up. Promise?"

"Don't play with me." She propped her

arms over her belly and began tapping her right foot, picking up the pace by the second, a sure sign that she was getting agitated.

When Dominique was on the verge of imploding, she started running her mouth, punctuated by perfectly placed cuss words. Desiree, on the other hand, would start with the pose and then foot tapping, eye-rolling and the barrage would follow. She hadn't gotten to the eye-rolling phase yet.

"Aunt J got a call . . . from Janae . . ." Rafe began.

By the time he'd finished bringing Desiree up to speed, her eyes had filled with tears of despair for her brother.

"Rafe," Desiree said with a catch in her throat. "My God, I don't even know what to say." She turned to her twin, who mirrored her distressed expression. "What about Avery? What did she say about you going to see Janae?"

"She doesn't know," he confessed.

"Rafe! You have to tell her," Desiree insisted. "How are you going to explain all this *after* the fact?"

"I'll handle it, Desi."

She reached out and took his hands. "You have to."

Rafe blew out a breath. "I will."

Desiree rubbed her belly and said, "Are you going to tell Justin?"

Rafe nodded. "Plan to. Might as well bring the whole family in on it. This . . . Janae thing affects all of us one way or another."

The trio walked back over to the veranda, where the rest of the family was intently listening to Raymond's story about one of his trips to Nigeria. All eyes turned in the direction of the three somber faces that approached.

Rafe stepped up onto the wood decking of the veranda and leaned against the railing. "I got some news," he began and gave his aunt a quick look . . .

The media and Janae. How long would it be before they latched onto *that* story? He had to tell Avery, but he needed to put his own eyes on Janae before he would really believe what he already knew. New York would wait; seeing Janae in Florida would not.

He walked over to the small desk tucked away in a corner of his bedroom, opened the cover of his laptop and signed in to the travel website that he used and booked a flight for Wednesday morning. He'd arrive in Miami at noon. That would give him the better part of the day to make sense out of this bittersweet nightmare.

He leaned back in the chair, gazed up at the ceiling and linked his fingers behind his head. What the hell was he going to do? Janae's parting words echoed in his head. She still loved him. But what about him? He was engaged to Avery. He loved *her.*

Frustration whipped through him, propelling him out of the chair to pace the bedroom floor. He wanted to see her again, desperately. What did that mean? What did that say about his feelings for Avery? He'd lost count of the nights he'd dreamed of Janae. There were so many versions of how he'd been able to save her. In some dreams they never made it to New York, but went to Atlanta instead. The only way to keep himself from losing his mind was to push her out of it. His stomach clenched. Admitting it, even to himself, only amplified his guilt. So, he did all he could not to think about Janae at all, what they'd had and the day that changed everything. He'd gotten good at it, good enough that he found space in his soul for Avery. Now . . .

He sat on the edge of his bed, looked across the room to the black backpack that held his things for his short trip to Florida. The Lawson clan vowed to be there for him for whatever he needed, whatever he decided. But they all emphatically agreed that he could not go to Florida before he spoke to Avery.

He knew they were right. That wasn't the issue. The issue that he'd been unwilling and unable to speak aloud was his unresolved feelings about Janae. He'd thought he'd finally put them to rest when he met Avery, but hearing her voice, knowing that she was still alive . . . He turned the phone around in his hand, ignored the knot of apprehension in his gut and placed a call to Quinten.

CHAPTER 13

"Yo, wait . . . what do you mean she's alive?" Quinten barked into the phone.

"Q, a woman claiming to be Janae called the house phone yesterday. Left a number for me to call in Florida. Knew stuff that only Janae would know. I called. I talked to her. It's got to be Janae."

"Damn," Quinten dragged out. "Whaddaya gonna do?"

Rafe paced the kitchen floor. "I booked a flight to Florida."

"What about Avery?"

Rafe ran down his plan.

Quinten sputtered an expletive from between his teeth.

Momentary silence hung between them.

"Hey, no way around it, bruh. Gotta know for sure," Quinten said. "And when you do, you will deal with things between you and Avery."

"Yeah. I know."

"Say the word and I can fly down there to ya. No problem."

"Naw. I'm good. I'll take care of it. See what she . . . has to say. Figure it out from there."

"I'm here if you need me."

"Thanks. I'll let you know what happened. Say hey to Rae for me."

"Will do. Easy, man."

"Yeah. Later."

"Damn, girl," Kerry whispered. "How in the world did they know where you were going to be?" She poured them both a glass of wine.

"Who the hell knows?" She paced her kitchen floor and vacillated between anger and defeat. She ran both hands through her hair. "This is my damned job, my career they're messing with! The director all but told me that I'll be on desk duty indefinitely. He can't risk my personal life jeopardizing the people I'm assigned to protect. He even suggested that maybe I should take a leave of absence." Her eyes burned with tears of fury.

Kerry muttered a curse. "This might not be the right question, but have you spoken with Rafe?"

She tossed her head back and laughed bitterly. "Rafe! Rafe! Him and his family are the reasons why this happening."

"I'll take that as a no," she muttered.

Avery cut her eyes in Kerry's direction. "What . . . you think I should call him, that he's going to ride in on his white horse and fix this mess?"

"No. But I do think he needs to know what's going on."

Avery plopped down on the kitchen chair. She gazed off into the distance. "He said he was going to take care of it, that all this would pass," she said, her voice weighed down with disappointment.

"I'm sure if there was anything that he could have personally done, he did, A."

Avery sighed heavily. "I don't even know anymore." She turned her pained eyes toward her friend. "I was totally humiliated today."

Kerry reached across the table and covered Avery's clenched fists with a comforting hand. "It's gonna be all right, girl. Ya'll love each other. You'll get through it together."

Avery sniffed, blinked back tears and reached for her glass of wine. "Yeah, until the next shoe drops."

"But until it does, which more than likely it will — simply because that's life — you need to talk to him and let him know what's going on."

Avery took a sip of her wine. "I will."

"Good." She pushed back from her seat and stood. "I gotta run. Date," she added with a half smile.

"Enjoy. I'll be fine. I promise I won't walk out into traffic." She forced a laugh.

"See you tomorrow."

"Okay. Thanks for coming by."

"I got you." She gathered her things and left. "I'll come by after. I can tell already that it's going to be an early night. Leave the key."

"You don't have to do that."

"I know." She pecked her cheek and left.

Avery stared at her cell phone. Once she'd finished her glass of wine, she reached for her phone. It rang in her hand.

CHAPTER 14

"Hey, darlin'," he gently greeted. "I need to talk to you . . ."

After he'd spilled his guts about the reappearance of Janae and his plans to fly out to see her, Avery was quiet for so long that at first he thought she'd hung up, until he heard what sounded like muffled sobs.

"Avery . . . cher . . . please don't cry . . . talk to me."

"What do you want me to say?" she finally managed. "You're stunned . . . confused . . . whatever. I get it," she said. The fire returned to her voice. "That's not what's killing me inside. What's killing me is that you lied to me, Rafe. You *knew* you were planning to see her and even if you didn't know for sure, you never said a word. I could tell something was wrong when we talked, but I convinced myself it was my imagination. You were going to let me believe you were going to New York. From everything you've *decided* to tell me, if it wasn't for your family, you might not have said a damned word! How am I supposed to marry a man that would lie to me? But the real question, the question that is turning my stomach is, why? Why would he lie to me? And none of the answers that I've come up with have me and you working out."

His whole body jerked in alarm. "Avery. Wait a second. Listen to me."

"No. I've heard enough. Have a safe trip. I hope it's everything you want it to be. Goodbye, Rafe."

The sound of the dial tone vibrated in his ear. He dialed her back. The call went to voice mail. He tried three consecutive times with the same result.

"What are you going to do?"

Avery propped her bare feet up on the circular ottoman and took a sip from her glass of wine. "Go to work tomorrow," she said and stared off into space. "Try to salvage what's left of my job."

"You know what I'm talking about, A," Kerry said.

Avery blew out a slow breath. "I can't marry a man that would lie to me. I can't marry a man that's still in love with someone else." She sniffed as tears threatened.

"Who says he's in love with her? Did he tell you that? Come on, Avery. What would you have done in the same situation? No one could have been more blown away about the woman coming back from the dead than he was. You know why you're doing this," she said softly.

"Doing what?"

"Running."

Avery turned her face away from the truth. "I'm not," she said without much conviction.

"You figure if you can cut ties first you won't be the last one standing. You stay in control."

Avery pressed her fist to her mouth.

"Do you love him?"

"You know I do!"

"Do you believe he loves you?"

She hesitated. "Yes," she whispered.

"Tell him that. He probably needs your support now more than ever."

"But what if he realizes that he's still in love with her?"

Kerry gave a sad shrug. "There's nothing that you can do about anyone else's feelings. If it's meant to be, Rafe is gonna come back here and marry you, just like the plan."

Avery swiped at her eyes. "And what if he doesn't?"

"You'll deal with it. You've never been a woman that needs a man to define her. None of that is gonna change, with or without Rafe Lawson."

Avery lowered her gaze and studied the remnants of her wine. This was something out of a novel, not real life. Her life was orderly, foreseeable. She was trained to spot trouble from yards away. She'd missed this one by a long shot. What would she do if Rafe told her that he was still in love with Janae? And was she really angry at Rafe for his deception, or angry at herself for the lie that she was perpetrating to everyone in her life?

The question trampled through her mind. Was she really willing to simply give up, let go of the man of her dreams and fold like a three-legged table? Kerry was right. Deep inside, part of her wanted to be the one to walk away, to end it. Love was the one challenge she was never able to conquer. Her love couldn't save her mother. Her love couldn't soften her father's heart. The two most important people in her life were lost to her. Their loss carved a hole in her spirit, made her believe she was unworthy and that love only led to hurt and emptiness.

Loving Rafe was so blinding, like looking into the sun. It consumed her, tricked her into believing that love could bring happiness and fulfillment. But in the end, it would end. It always did.

Kerry rubbed sleep from her eyes and robotically fixed a pot of coffee. When Avery's bell rang she thought she was hearing things, until it rang again. Early morning visits and late-night calls were always trouble.

She tightened the belt on her robe and went to the door. She peeked through the blinds on the window next to the door. Her mouth dropped open. She glanced over her shoulder, back at the door and unlocked it. She pulled the door open and stood like a sentinel.

"Kerry."

"What are you doing here?" she demanded.

"I need to see Avery."

"Really? *Now* you need to see her?"

"Kerry, is she here?"

She folded her arms in defiance. "You have no idea what you did — what you did to her."

"That's why I'm here, because I do know," he said quietly.

Kerry's chest rose and fell. She glared at him for a moment longer and then stepped aside and let him in.

"Thank you."

The door shut behind him. "Have a seat. I'll go —"

They both looked toward the stairs.

Avery gripped the bannister. When he looked into her eyes in that way that flipped her heart, for a moment she forgot what was wrong, all the crap that happened in the last twenty-four hours, and all she wanted to do was run to him. But she didn't.

"You want me to stay?" Kerry asked.

"No. It's okay." She came down the final step and walked into the living room. "Why are you here, Rafe?"

"I needed to see you, cher."

Her insides shifted. She bit down on her bottom lip, crossed the room and sat on the side chair to keep him from sitting next to her, so that she could think — breathe.

Rafe was not going to make it easy. He came to her, knelt in front of her and took her hands in his.

"Forgive me."

She blinked rapidly against the burn of tears that threatened to fall.

He squeezed her hands, lifted one to his lips and kissed the inside of her palm. "Forgive me, cher. I never wanted to hurt you, deceive you. Never. I should have told you everything that I knew when I knew it. Yes, I planned to go and see her without telling you. Not because I wanted to lie to you, but because I wanted to be sure before I brought my baggage and asked you to unpack it." The ache in his voice reached his eyes as they moved inch by inch across her face and dipped down into her soul. "I love *you*. You."

She would put an end to all this, and tell him it was too late, that he should leave. *Now.* But she needed something different for herself. She needed to stop being afraid of tumbling into love, and allow it into her heart. For real. If there was anyone she could take that big leap with, she believed it was Rafe Lawson.

Slowly she nodded her head, wiped at her eyes. "I love you," she said in a shaky whisper.

"That's all we need." He rose from his knees and gently pulled her to her feet, took her face in his large hands. He lowered his head and covered her lips with his.

Her sigh mixed with his moan of relief and need.

"I'm sorry, cher," he whispered against her mouth before dipping his tongue into the sweetness of her mouth.

Her arms looped around his neck, and his

clasped around her back and waist and pulled her fully against his rising desire.

"Come home with me," he said, his voice hot with desire.

She leaned back to look into his eyes. "New Orleans?"

"Arlington."

She held onto the smile blooming on her lips. "Oh." She tipped her head to the right side. "And what would we be doing at your home in Arlington? A girl has to get to work in the morning." Such that it was. But they had enough to deal with. She'd deal with her own issues.

"I'll make sure you get to work and ready to take on all the bad guys." His thumb brushed her bottom lip. "Say yes. I want you. Can't you tell?"

His slow easy grin ignited the smoldering flame in her center to a four-alarm blaze.

"You are a charmer, Rafe Lawson," she purred. "I finish at five. I can be to you by six."

He hung his hands on her waist. "I'll send Alice home and fix dinner myself."

"Okay."

The loud clearing of Kerry's throat had them both turn in her direction. She was fully dressed and leaning against the frame of the archway.

"I can only conclude that whatever needed to be worked out got worked out. But . . ." She focused on Avery. "You're going to be late."

"Oh no. What time is it?"

"6:15."

She looked at Rafe with apology written all over her face. "I'm sorry. I've got to get ready."

"Yeah, yeah. Go. I'll see you later." He kissed her one last time as if they were the only two people in the world. "Six." He released her and walked toward the front door. "Thanks," he quietly said to Kerry as he passed her. The door closed softly behind him.

"All is forgiven I take it?" Kerry asked, turning toward Avery.

Avery blew out a breath, still wrapped in the essence of Rafe. "I . . . we'll see." She looked at her friend. "I want to try. I need to."

"Did you tell him what happened at work?"

"No. I'll figure it out on my own. Like you said, it'll work out."

"Good. But, girl." She turned her head toward the closed door. "If that man came for me, I'm going with him. I'm just saying. Humph."

140

Avery burst out laughing and draped her arm across Kerry's shoulder. "I know that's right."

Even though she was temporarily stuck behind a desk, it wasn't as awful as she'd thought. There was plenty to keep her busy. At least she had something wonderful to look forward to at the end of her shift. The director had reassigned her to scheduling — from detail assignments to training and mapping where every agent was and with whom. It was one of those detail-oriented assignments that she was actually quite skilled at.

Toward the end of the day she was summoned to the director's office. She braced herself for more bad news.

"Come in and have a seat, Agent Richards."

Avery sat. Was this the other shoe? She lifted her chin and focused on the director.

"I've had an opportunity to consider what transpired at the Watergate. I'm fully aware that it was not of your making. You're a damned good agent. One of our best. But what happened could have seriously jeopardized the safety and security of your charge."

"Yes, sir." She continued to look him

square in the eye.

"There is no easy solution."

Her heart began to race.

"For the next month I want you off detail. You'll work in-house. Give the vultures time to set their sights on something else. When I feel it's appropriate I'll see about getting you back out into active field duty."

She swallowed. "Yes, sir."

Director Fischer linked his thick fingers together on top of the desk. "We should be making a decision on the promotion in the next month or so. Keeping you out of the headlines will help in that arena." He cleared his throat. "I will be honest with you, Agent Richards, the hiring committee is very concerned that with you marrying someone of such high profile, it may be a major liability. We're weighing all the options."

She kept her expression neutral. "Thank you, sir."

He nodded solemnly. "Keep doing a good job, Agent Richards."

"I will, sir. Thank you." She rose, turned and left. She tried not to let her anxiety show on her face as she passed several colleagues in the corridor. She was still being considered. At least that was something. She beat down the ugly feeling of resentment.

Why should falling in love possibly cost her everything she'd worked for? One thing that she could count on was that Rafe would make her forget all the things she didn't want to think about.

When Avery arrived at Rafe's home, neither wasted any time. Rafe greeted her with a kiss that weakened her knees, plied her with a chilled glass of wine and then lulled her to a scented bath. He took great pleasure in undressing her, of rediscovering the rose-petal softness of her skin before he helped her into the deep jet tub.

He knelt down next to her as she sank into the steamy, scented water. She sighed, her body and mind succumbing to pure bliss. Rafe took the blue sponge and gently washed her back, squeezing the hot, sudsy water over her shoulders and down the rise of her breasts, which peeked out above the water. He leaned in and kissed her on the back of her neck. "Want some company?" he whispered. He nibbled her ear while his free hand wandered across the swell of her breast, before diving down into the water between her legs.

Avery drew in a quick breath as his thumb brushed across her swelling clit. "I'd . . . love it."

Rafe stood and tugged his fitted black T-shirt over his head, tossed it aside. He pulled on the string of his gray sweatpants and let them pool at his feet.

Avery's breath stopped in her chest, awed as always by the sheer perfection of his milk-chocolate body coming into full view. Her teeth taunted her bottom lip while she watched him, over her shoulder, step into the tub and ease down. His long, muscular legs straddled either side of her. She felt his growing erection press against her lower back.

Rafe lifted the thick, wild spirals of her hair from her neck and placed hot kisses there and down along her spine. His arms looped around her waist, fanned out and separated her thighs. "Bend your knees," he whispered in her ear. "And lean back against me."

She glanced at him over her shoulder and caught the glint of fire in his eyes. She bent her knees and leaned back.

His large hands slid up and down the inside of her thighs, the water making the path smooth as silk. His fingers spread across her belly and up to the underside of her breasts before sliding back into the water to brush and tease her exposed clit.

Avery whimpered. Her body trembled

ever so slightly.

Rafe eased her further down toward the faucets. He cupped her breasts and teased the taut nipples until her moans rose in shuddering bursts.

Avery rested her head against his chest, closed her eyes and succumbed to his pleasuring.

"Rest your heels on either side of the tub," Rafe ground out.

Avery followed his instructions.

He eased her forward a bit more until she was spread wide and vulnerable. He clasped her tightly around the waist and turned on the jets. The warm water gushed out and felt like a million massaging fingers. The intensity of the onslaught of rushing water against her fully exposed, totally stimulated clit made her see stars.

"Ohhhh!"

"Hmmm, relax . . . enjoy," he cooed, holding her in place.

Rafe reached around and held her thighs firmly apart. The water pulsed steadily against her. Her limbs trembled. Her moans turned to whimpers. She gripped the side of the tub. Her breathing escalated as mind-altering pleasure whipped through her.

"Go with it, darlin'," he whispered.

She struggled to breathe as the first wave

crashed against her. Her cry mixed with the steam-scented air. Rafe slipped two fingers inside of her, and lights burst behind her eyes.

"Ahhhh, ahhhh!" Her hips rose and fell, thrashed against his hand and the power of the water as jolts of pleasure roared through her veins. Shudders ran up and down her body as wave after wave of release erupted until she was weak.

Avery smiled as she listened to Rafe singing in off-key splendor in the kitchen while she tugged the sheets off the bed and straightened up his bedroom the following morning. She shoved the sheets inside of a pillowcase and went to the walk-in closet to get a clean set, and nearly tripped over what Rafe called his "go-bag." She picked it up to put it on the shelf, out of the way, and a folded set of papers fell out on the floor. She reached down to pick them up and noticed the lawyer letterhead. She didn't consider herself a snoop in the sense that she went around looking for things, but her instincts kicked in and she opened the papers.

She frowned as the words spilled out in front of her. The more she read, the more furious she became. A prenuptial agreement! She couldn't believe that Rafe would do something like this — to *her*. Did he think she was some kind of gold digger who was only after him for his money! What the hell.

Her temple began to pound.

"Hey, cher, I whipped us up some —"

"What is this?" She waved the papers in front of him. "A damned prenup, Rafe. Are you kidding me?"

Rafe held up his hands. "Take it easy."

"Easy! Easy! No. I won't take it easy." She paced in front of him. "Isn't it enough that your family tried to hijack the wedding and, for all intents and purposes, I've been demoted to desk duty because of the damned press following me around. That's my life, my career that I built. On hold. And let's not forget your ex-lover that has risen from the dead!" Her eyes filled with tears. "And now this!" She shook the pages violently in the air and then threw them on the floor. She slowly shook her head. "I'm the one that has had to adapt, change, give things up. Me." Her chest heaved with emotion. "I can't do this." Her throat clenched.

His countenance tightened. "What are you saying?"

She faced him. Tears ran down her cheeks. "I can't do this . . . I can't marry you."

"Avery." He took a step toward her. She held up her hand to halt him.

"Marrying you . . . I'd gain a husband but lose myself. Between your family and that," she pointed to the papers on the floor, "and . . . my career going down in flames . . ." She swiped at her eyes. "I can't." She looked down at the diamond blazing on her finger. She twisted the band and slid the ring from her finger.

Rafe stared at her. Stunned. Hurt. But shock was quickly replaced with anger. "I should have known better. I should have kept living my life. *My* damned life! Whatever made me think that this would be different?" He snorted a sound of disgust. "Well, you got your wish. This is what you wanted all along — a way out. You got it." He stared at her hard. "Keep the ring." He whirled away, stormed down the hall and out.

The door rattled in its frame. The next sound she heard was the roar of his motorcycle.

She stood under the arch of the closet door, gripped the diamond in her palm, slipped to her knees and wept.

Dazed, spent, she finally pulled herself together, gathered her things and left Rafe's

148

home. She couldn't go home, didn't want to. She went to Kerry's place in DC, instead. She was numb as she moved through the space like a ghost — disembodied from the real world.

What had she done? Rafe was right. She had been looking for a way out and he provided her with all the ammunition she needed. Her secret, her fear of what might really be wrong with her, drove her decision. If she was honest with herself, she knew that to be true. Rafe had been down the road of losing someone before and it nearly broke him. She couldn't do that to him again. It was best this way. Her head pounded. She pressed the heels of her palms against her eyes. Her shoulders shook as sobs overtook her again.

When Kerry came home several hours later she was beyond surprised to see her friend curled up on the love seat.

"Hey there, I didn't expect you back." She tossed her purse on the couch. "Where's Rafe?" She pulled off her jacket and added it to the couch.

Avery curled into an even tighter knot on the love seat.

"A, what's going on?"

She slowly lifted her chin from her chest. "It's over. The wedding is off."

"What are you talking about?" She plopped down on the side chair. "What happened?"

In bits and pieces Avery told Kerry about the prenup, the fight and her declaration. For quite some time after she'd finished, Kerry sat in silence. Finally she spoke.

"What is really going on, Avery? This isn't about a piece of paper."

"Yes, it is," she insisted.

"Don't b.s. me. I'm your friend. You love that man. And he loves you. You were willing to go the extra mile when he explained about Janae. But you freak out over a piece of paper. Are you serious?"

"It's not going to work." She shook her head. "There are too many obstacles and we aren't even married yet."

Kerry covered her face with her hands and groaned as if in agony. She pulled her hands away and jumped up from her seat. "This is nonsense."

"No, it —"

"Yes, it is, and you damn well know it." She huffed out a breath. "Do you love him?" She stared at her friend, daring her to lie.

"Yes."

"Do you believe he loves you?"

Avery swallowed. "Yes."

"Does he make you happy?"

"Yes." Avery lowered her head, linked her fingers together and studied her bare feet.

"Do you know how lucky you are? You have a man that adores you, a family willing to make you a part of it — something you've never had. Not only does that man love you, he's smart, talented, gorgeous, sexy *and* rich."

Avery sniffed. She drew in a long breath, pursed her lips and released the truth that she'd been battling with for months.

"There's something I need to tell you . . ."

CHAPTER 15

Rafe was blind with hurt and fury. He tore through the streets of Virginia like a man possessed. Avery had no idea all that he'd given up for her, everything that he was willing to change for her. He'd opened his heart and his soul, something he'd vowed never to do again. He could have told her that the prenup wasn't his idea and that he'd planned to confront his father. But why should he have to try to convince the woman who was supposed to love him that the man she'd decided he was could never be the man that he knew himself to be? No.

He raced by an eighteen-wheeler to the blare of angry horns and screeching tires. He'd thought they'd gotten over the biggest hurdle thrown at them — Janae — or at least someone claiming to be her.

Janae would have given him a chance to explain. Janae listened. She always listened. *Avery* . . . He pressed down on the accelerator, cut across two lanes of traffic and zipped onto the exit to downtown DC.

He parked his bike in front of the only available space on the street. He looked up at the awning. *Baldwin's.* He snorted a disgusted laugh at the irony the beginning and the end.

Rafe pushed through the doors of Baldwin's and the quick flow of memories rushed at him. He went straight to the bar, determined to wash the images away.

The club, generally packed in the evening, was loosely occupied with early lunch goers who flocked there for the midday slider special, which was fine with him. He wanted to be by himself but not totally alone. He knew how quickly he could sink into that dark place, and being at home with nothing to distract him would take him there via express.

"What can I get you?"

Rafe looked up. *Pretty* was his first thought. "Bourbon."

"Straight up?"

"Yeah, thanks. Make it a double. Please."

He slightly swiveled his head to follow her movements. He felt like he knew her from somewhere but couldn't quite recall. She returned moments later and set the short tumbler of bourbon in front of him.

"Can I get you a menu?"

He gave a short shrug. "Sure."

She reached beneath the counter and pulled out a menu. "Take your time. Let me know when you're ready." She went to tend to another customer.

Rafe lifted the glass to his lips and took a deep swallow. The liquid heat hit his empty belly like a splash of lava. He breathed in deeply, let the warmth flow through his limbs. He wrapped his hands around the glass and stared off at nothing in particular. The light chatter of the customers and activity of the staff faded around him.

He'd truly believed that Avery was the one. After years of running, hiding from commitment after Janae, he was ready to let go of the past hurt and loss and begin a life with Avery. But even from the beginning, as much as he believed she cared for him, there was a part of her that he never seemed to reach. But he'd chalked it up to his own battle with personal demons. He finished his drink. Obviously, his instincts were right.

He wasn't sure what was driving the rage inside him: the idea that it was so easy for her to throw everything they had away, or the idea that she somehow believed the worst of him.

Probably best. He signaled for a refill.

Maybe Janae's resurrection was more than bad timing, maybe . . . Naw, he wouldn't go down that road. Until he put his own eyes on her, he couldn't be sure of anything. That was the craziest part of this ugly day. Avery seemed willing to understand about Janae, and his need to see her, but was ready to toss everything out the window over a prenup that he had nothing to do with.

"Here you go. Ready to order?"

Rafe's dark gaze lifted to settle on her face. Recognition nipped around the edges, but would not come full bloom.

"I used to work with Bailey at the Meridian," she said with a knowing half smile. "Addy. I worked your grandfather's birthday party last year with her, too."

Rafe snapped his fingers. "That's where!" His smile slowly dissolved. *The night he met Avery.* "Was racking my brain trying to place you. What are you doing here?"

"Got married six months ago and we moved here for my husband's job. He teaches at the University of Virginia."

"Nice."

"How's Bailey?"

"She's great. Saw her last week, when I was back home."

"We kind of lost touch when she moved to New York with Justin."

155

Avery wouldn't have relocated to New Orleans for him, even though he'd been willing, much like his brother Justin, who uprooted his life for the woman he loved. He finished off his second drink as the dark clouds loomed closer.

"You're a long way from home yourself."

"Here on business." His jaw tightened. "How 'bout another refill." He held up his empty glass.

"You know we have the best crab cake sliders this side of the Mississippi. Why don't I bring you a plate with that next drink?"

He half grinned. "Sure thing." He grabbed a handful of mini pretzels from the glass bowl she'd subtly put in front of him, and tossed them in his mouth. He chewed thoughtfully, thinking about relationships that were his examples: his sisters and their husbands, his aunt Jacquie and Raymond, Justin and Bailey, and even his father and mother, when she was alive. They were all willing to sacrifice a part of themselves for the person they'd committed themselves to. That's what he'd been willing to offer Avery, beyond his body, his soul, his fortune. Obviously she didn't feel the same way.

Addy returned with his food and his refill. "Need anything else, let me know."

"Wish it was that easy, darlin'," he said into his glass. "Wish it was."

Addy made sure he was good and sober before he left Baldwin's nearly three hours after his arrival. He could tell the drinks had grown weaker as the pretzel bowl grew larger and was topped off by two cups of coffee.

"I want to thank you for a very pleasant afternoon," he said after paying his tab. "I'm pretty sure you're the reason I won't be a stain on the street."

"You just be careful out there, and I hope whatever is bothering you works itself out."

He pushed to his feet. "I'm sure it will one way or the other. Always does." He winked.

"Take care."

"You, too."

Addy walked to the other end to serve a customer. Rafe reached into his pocket for his wallet, returned his credit card and took out a hundred-dollar bill. He wrote "thank you" and placed it under the pretzel bowl.

He stepped out into the late afternoon sunshine, glanced back at the awning. Baldwin's. He shook his head, hopped on his bike and revved the engine. Hopefully Avery would be long gone by the time he returned. He needed to get ready for his trip to Florida and finally clear his plate of the distant and soon-to-be past so that he could move on.

CHAPTER 16

"I'm listening," Kerry said while she settled on the paisley printed side chair.

"I haven't been honest . . . about my health."

Kerry sat straighter. "What are you talking about? You said the doctors cleared you."

"Only because I haven't told them what's been going on with the headaches."

Kerry frowned.

"They haven't gone away. Sometimes they are almost blinding." She paused. "I stopped taking the pain meds for a while before my physical so there would be no drugs in my blood."

Kerry hung her head and then looked across at her friend. "Why?" She held up her hand. "Don't tell me — because of this damned job." She blew out a breath of frustration. "Are you crazy! Over a job. Seriously? What good is it going to do if you pass out or worse?"

Avery worried her bottom lip with her teeth. "My job, my career — it's everything that I've worked for. Can't you see that?"

"What I see is someone willing to sacrifice their health and maybe their life for a job that will replace you in a heartbeat with a plaque on the wall. Not to mention that you could be putting everyone around you in jeopardy if you have one of those episodes on duty. I know how important this promotion is for you. It's a chance to prove something to your father."

Avery looked away.

"But, girl!"

"I was scared. I *am* scared that it's something more than the after effects of the explosion." She blinked slowly. "It's the real reason why I broke it off with Rafe."

"What? What are you talking about?"

Avery curled up tighter in the chair. "Rafe has already lost so much. Everyone in his family told me what losing Janae did to him."

"Yeah, but apparently she ain't lost," she snapped.

"That's not the point."

"Then what is? 'Cause I don't get it."

Avery dropped her bare feet to the floor and leaned forward. "If something is really wrong with me . . . something serious, I can't saddle him with that. I won't."

"You're being very . . . *Avery.* Stubborn and single-focused. That man loves you. You love him."

"It's not enough."

"Hell if it ain't. Sickness and in health."

"*After* the 'I dos.' "

"You don't even know what's really wrong. For all you know, it could be the medication, or your recovery time is just longer than they thought. It could be a bunch of things."

Avery wiped a tear away.

"I can't let you do this. You're going to the doctor and let them run whatever tests they need to run. And we'll deal with whatever. As for Rafe, that part is up to you, but going to the doctor is not up for debate. I'm going with you."

"Okay," she conceded. "As long as you come with me."

"Not a problem. Make the appointment." She stood. "You're staying here tonight."

Avery nodded.

"I'm going to see what's in the fridge, or we can order." As she passed Avery she squeezed her shoulder. "It's going to be okay."

Avery stared off into the distance. What if it wasn't?

161

■ ■ ■ ■

"Please stow away any electronics, put tray tables up and ensure that your seat belt is locked. We will be landing in the Sunshine State shortly, where the weather is a balmy 80 degrees."

The flight attendant's announcement clicked off. Rafe gazed out the window as the landscape of Florida began to break through the puffs of white.

He'd barely slept the night before, leaving his mind and body on edge. When he'd returned home, there was a space in his soul that wanted Avery to be there to fill it. But the larger space, that dark hole that had begun to spread, was glad that she wasn't.

The plane bumped down on the tarmac and cruised to the gate. Rafe unsnapped his seat belt, got up and retrieved his carryon from the overhead, and then helped a young mother who was trying to juggle a sleeping baby and two bags.

"Here, let me help," Rafe offered and gently took the bags and draped them over his shoulder.

"Thank you so much," she breathed in relief. "I think my son must have gained five pounds while he slept," she joked. She peered down at the baby's innocent face.

"He slept the whole trip," Rafe commented, walking down the aisle, behind the woman.

"He is an angel. Never gives me a minute of trouble and he loves to travel." She laughed lightly and kissed the baby's forehead.

They exited the plane and walked out into the arrival terminal.

"Do you have luggage?"

"No, but my husband is meeting me in baggage claim."

"So, you live here?" They walked side by side through the throng of travelers.

"Yes. About five years. Originally from New York. My husband's mom got ill so we relocated here. You?"

"Visiting. From New Orleans."

She smiled. "I thought I heard a little twang," she teased.

Rafe chuckled. "I should have picked up on the New *Yawk*."

She wagged a finger and grinned. "I told my husband that we may have moved South but I was keeping my New Yawk accent."

They entered the baggage claim area and headed for the exit. She peeked over heads and between bodies and then suddenly her face lit up. She raised her arm and waved.

"There he is."

A tall, medium-built man in a white T-shirt and khaki shorts came toward them, but it was clear that he only had eyes for his wife and son.

The instant they were close enough his fingers threaded through her Angela Davis afro and pulled her in for a long "find a room" kiss.

Rafe lowered his gaze until the couple reluctantly separated. Their son was wide awake now and apparently just as happy to see his father as his mother was, as he began to bounce in his mother's arms and reached for his father. The man lifted his son into his arms.

The scene in front of Rafe was simple, happened every day, but for him it hit his gut in a way that saddened him. This was what he'd hoped for — to have his own family to come home to. Maybe this kind of life wasn't in the cards for him. That realization broke something inside him.

The woman turned toward Rafe. "I am so sorry. Sweetie, this nice man helped me with my bags. I didn't even ask your name."

"Rafe Lawson."

"Thanks, man," the husband said and shook Rafe's hand before taking the two bags from him. "Glen Dawkins, and you've met my wife, Selena, and our son, Gabriel," he said, sliding his arm around the waist of his wife.

"Pleasure."

"Thanks again," Selena said. "Enjoy your stay."

Rafe offered a tight-lipped smile, gave a short nod to the couple and walked away. He couldn't imagine that enjoyment would factor into his visit.

Once outside, he called for an Uber, and a half hour later, he was in his hotel room at the *W*.

Rafe sat on the side of the king-size bed that faced the beach. From the panoramic window of his fifteenth-floor suite the pulsing expanse of Miami Beach spread out before him. Any other time he would be planning his night out on the town; instead he was mulling over the inevitable. He stared at the face of his cell phone, used his thumb print to open the screen and scrolled for the number stored for Janae. He looked at it, tossed the phone across the bed. Not yet.

Rafe stood, walked to the window and opened the terrace doors. He leaned on the railing and inhaled the scent of ocean air.

Why put off calling Janae? It was the only reason he was in Florida. But to see her, confirm for himself that the voice on the phone was truly Janae, would upend everything he'd believed and grown to accept all these years. Where would that leave him — them?

He turned away from the setting sun and returned inside. He picked up the phone from the bed. This time he dialed her number.

"Hello?"

"It's Rafe."

"Hi," she said with that same sweet inflection that he remembered.

Rafe closed his eyes for a moment. "I'm in town. Only overnight. I thought we could meet tomorrow."

"Yes," she said almost before he could finish.

"Where?"

"You can come here if you don't mind."

"Text me the address. Noon work for you?"

"Fine. I'll see you then."

"Tomorrow, then."

Rafe disconnected the call and realized that his pulse was racing. He dragged in a breath, looked at his screen again, swiped for his messages and snorted a derisive laugh. Nothing from Avery.

His phone chirped with an incoming message. *Janae's address.* He slid the phone into his pocket, picked up his room card key from the dresser and went in search of the bar.

CHAPTER 17

"Ready?" Kerry asked while she checked the contents of her purse.

"As ready as I can be."

"I'm just glad the doctor was able to see you on such short notice."

"Guess he heard the low-level panic in my voice. He wants me to go straight to the diagnostic center for the CAT scan, then come to his office."

Kerry walked over to where Avery stood, putting on her jacket. She put her arm around the shoulder of her friend. "I know you're scared, but it's going to be okay. I feel it. But you have to believe it, too. And no matter what the doctor says, we'll deal with it. I'm here for you."

Avery's luminous brown eyes welled with tears. She pressed her lips tightly together and nodded her head.

"And you're going to talk to Rafe. Tell him the truth. He deserves it."

Avery glanced away, took her purse from the hall table. "I'll think about it. Rafe is busy reconnecting with his lost love."

"You know that's not what's going on. It's what you want to be going on so that you have a way out — blame him so that you won't have to tell him that you've been lying to him."

Avery jammed the straps of her purse over her shoulder. "I know what I'm doing," she snapped and walked to the front door.

"No, you don't," she muttered.

Avery tossed her a "not today" look over her shoulder. Kerry stuck out her tongue.

"I carry a gun too, ya know."

Avery huffed and stifled a chuckle. Kerry knew her better than she knew herself and always had a way of making her see the light, even when she didn't want to.

"I'll call him," Avery said, barely above a whisper, once they were seated and belted in Kerry's Honda.

Kerry lifted a brow. "Good."

"*After* I get the results back." She held up her hand to stop the retort she knew was coming.

Kerry put the car in gear and pulled out of her driveway. "Fine."

Avery didn't realize just how frightened she was until the nurse told her to get undressed and put on the gown, and that the doctor had ordered an MRI rather than the CAT scan. She knew instantly that the reason for the change was the doctor was concerned that something was missed on her earlier CAT scans. MRIs produced much more powerful images that revealed issues deep in tissue and bone.

She wanted to run out and just say the hell with it. But she knew she couldn't go on this way. She wanted her life back, free of pain and fear. Besides, she'd never get past Kerry, who was sitting in the reception area, waiting for her.

She hung up her clothes and put on the gown. A few moments later the nurse came to take her to the exam room. The tube-like contraption looked like something out of *Star Wars.*

The technician helped her onto the table and positioned her.

"This will take a while," the technician said. "And the noise can be unsettling, but I need you to remain as still as possible. We don't want to have to do this a second time." He made some adjustment to the panels on the tube and then left the room.

Moments later she heard the voice of the technician. "Ready to begin. Please don't move."

Avery closed her eyes, tried to tune out the rhythmic metallic bang of the machine and said a prayer.

CHAPTER 18

Rafe crossed the expansive lobby of the W hotel and stepped out into the blazing sunshine and pulsing energy of Miami. The Audi convertible rental that he'd picked up at the airport was driven to the front door of the hotel by the valet.

"Your keys, Mr. Lawson," the valet said.

"Thanks." He took a twenty from his wallet and pressed it into the young man's hand.

"Thank you, sir. Thank you."

Rafe gave a quick lift of his chin in acknowledgment and got behind the wheel of the Audi. He adjusted the mirrors and the seat to accommodate his height, punched in the address on the GPS, put the car in gear and drove off.

He'd been to Miami a few times over the years, mostly to party along South Beach, which is known for its glamorous nightspots and celebrity-chef eateries. He'd lost track of high-end stores and indie fashion shops he patronized that lined the shopping strip on Lincoln Road Mall. So, between the parties at night and the beach during the day, he really didn't pay much attention to street signs and landmarks. But from what he could recall, not much had changed since his last visit.

The streets, even before noon, were teeming with a montage of revelers, many of whom looked like they were coming in from the night before and others just getting started.

Rafe took Ocean Drive to the A1A. According to the GPA, he should arrive at Janae's place in twenty minutes. Staying focused on the building traffic helped to keep his thoughts off what he was heading toward. But every time traffic slowed to a halt, a flash of Janae would jump in front of him.

He was so torn between simmering anger at the deception that had gone on for more than sixteen years, and the unresolved feelings he'd buried that had begun to bubble to the surface.

Her house was less than five minutes away. He took the next exit and drove along Orchard Road and began checking addresses. Number 5856. He slowed and turned the car onto the short driveway and pulled up to the single-story home. The large bay windows wrapped around either side of the front door, which was covered by a portico. The lawn looked freshly mowed and the shrubbery clipped with precision. A single towering palm stood sentinel.

For several moments Rafe sat behind the wheel, gripping it with both hands. The house didn't look like anything he'd ever imagine for Janae. But then again, he no longer knew *this* Janae. He turned off the engine. There was no turning back. Whatever happened on the other side of the door, he'd deal with.

The front door opened in concert with him stepping out of the car. For an instant the world stopped spinning. It was her, in the flesh, and not her at the same time. His heart hammered so hard in his chest that it was difficult to breathe. And then she smiled. It *was* Janae. He would never forget the smile that lit up every corner it touched.

Caught in the surreal moment he slowly walked down the rest of the driveway and stopped at the bottom step.

"Rafe . . ."

Her hair was long now, framing and hiding her face at the same time, not like the short twists she once wore that showcased her wide eyes and high cheekbones.

He came up the two steps to stand in front of her. "Janae."

"Thank you for coming."

He jammed his hands in his pockets.

"Come in." She stepped aside and held the screen door open.

Rafe eased by her and entered the small foyer that opened on either side to the sitting room on the left and kitchen to the right. From where he stood he could see straight out to the back that boasted a small pool — a staple of Florida living.

"We can talk in here," Janae said, extending her arm toward the sitting room.

He followed her and couldn't help but notice the slight limp as she walked. Inwardly he winced for her pain. He took a quick look around. The room was small, but cozy and a bit overstuffed with knickknacks and memorabilia that took up the mantel, glass cabinets and end tables. Framed photos of Janae with her parents hung on the walls.

Rafe turned to face her. He unbuttoned the single button on his navy-blue sports jacket, revealing the brilliant white open-collared shirt.

"Can I get you anything? Something to drink?"

"No. I'm fine. Thanks." He sat in the armchair near the window.

Janae took her time and sat opposite him. A circular table separated them.

"Where do I begin?" she said softly.

"Anywhere. Tell me something that makes sense, Janae. When you remembered something, anything about us, why didn't you let me know you were alive? How could you do that to someone that you claimed to love?" He leaped up out of his seat and began to pace, rubbing his hand across the back of his neck. He whirled toward her.

"It was *because* I loved you that I didn't call," she said, so quietly that it sounded like a prayer. "I had so many physical struggles after what happened — still do. Memory pretty much gone, scars, nightmares." She sucked in a breath. "I didn't want to burden you, and my parents — my caretakers — convinced me that it was best for everyone that I stay away."

"Even if I was to accept that then, why now? Why come back now and ruin my life all over again?"

"I still love you, Rafe." Her deep bronze gaze pierced the protective coating he'd submerged himself in.

His gut shifted. Slowly he shook his head in denial. "It's not that simple anymore, J. I had no choice but to move on." His throat clenched while he slowly lowered himself into the chair. He rested his forearms on his muscled denim-clad thighs and leaned forward. "I can't even imagine everything you've been through, Janae. Sometimes I think that what I imagined was even more horrific — simply because I didn't know!" He linked his fingers together and looked into her eyes. "Maybe there's a part of me that understands all your reasons, but it doesn't take away all the damage that not knowing has done. In sixteen years, it was hard, but I moved on, Janae. I had no choice if I was gonna survive. Losing you . . . nearly destroyed me. I had to find my way without you, push into the back of my mind all the plans we made, the things we'd hoped for." He dragged in a breath. He thought about Avery — his second chance — and their last conversation. His jaw tightened. He wouldn't give in and let go again.

"Janae . . . I know I'll always love you, too." He breathed deeply. "But what we had is the past. I can't go back. *We* can't go back."

Janae lowered her head to hide the tears welling in her eyes. "I hoped . . ." She sniffed. "But I understand. I only want you to be happy, Rafe."

They were quiet for a moment. "What about your parents?" he gently probed.

She blinked rapidly. "They passed away. A year apart from each other about three years ago. I always believed they hung on to make sure that I was okay."

"I'm so sorry, Janae. Really."

She pressed her lips together and nodded slowly. "Thank you."

"So . . . you're here alone?" He studied her face and noticed for the first time the slight discoloration of her right cheek that looked as if it might be the result of burns.

"In the house, yes. But I have friends and my work. I do intervention at the local high school for at-risk students and double duty as guidance counselor."

He smiled, remembering her passion for social work. "That's great. I know you're amazing."

The stiffness of her shoulders seemed to finally relax, and a true smile lit her eyes. "I love my students. So many of them have it rough. I mean really rough." She looked right at him. "Not like how me and you grew up. We thought a hard time was not going to a concert, or the car not starting." They both laughed at the memories they shared. She glanced down at her hands, covered the left that was scarred. "I found my place. That part is good. I've made friends and have pieced together my life one day at a time." She swallowed. "There are still things that I don't clearly remember." She shrugged lightly. "I've grown to accept it and don't fight with myself about it anymore. It took time and a lot of therapy." She smiled, the way he remembered.

As he listened the hardened shell that he'd wrapped around that part of his soul that contained all things Janae slowly softened, and he allowed himself the briefest of moments to remember what it felt like to love her, but also the emotional work that it took to move on.

"I'm happy for you. I can't imagine your struggle, but the woman that I remember was always a fighter."

He stood. Janae's gaze rose with him. He came to her, took her hand and brought it to his lips. "Thank you for finally closing the space in my life, Janae. Knowing that you survived . . ." His throat tightened.

She stood, wrapped her arms around him and rested her head on his chest. He stroked her back and for a moment all the years and uncertainly slipped away. He stepped back. "Take care of yourself, Janae." He kissed

her cheek, turned away and didn't look
back.

CHAPTER 19

"We should have the results back from the radiologist in a day or so," the doctor said. "The pain, in the meantime, can be managed. I'm going to write you a new prescription. But you must take the medication."

Avery nodded. "Are there any side effects?"

"Well, it can make you groggy. You shouldn't drive for up to two hours after you take it."

"That's going to interfere with my job. I have to drive and be alert."

"Ms. Richards, I need you to understand that we can't ever be too cautious with head injuries. Most times they heal on their own, but sometimes they don't. I need you to be prepared for that. Hopefully, that won't be the case."

"Are you saying that I might be on some kind of medication for the rest of my life?" she asked, panic rising in her voice.

"It's possible. But let's not go down that road until we get the results back," he said, patting the air with his hand. "I'll give you a call as soon as I get the results. We'll go from there." He turned to his computer and tapped in her information. "The prescription is being sent to your pharmacy. It should be ready by the time you get back home." He folded his beefy hands on top of the desk. "Do you have any more questions for me?"

Avery lowered her head and shook it slowly. "No." She looked across the desk at him and then stood. "Thank you, Dr. Ryan."

Kerry popped up from her seat the moment Avery exited the doctor's office. "What did he say?"

"The results should be back in a day or two. Got a new prescription and was told that this may be my life," she added morosely.

"It's going to be okay. I know it will." She hooked her arm through Avery's as they walked out.

"Yeah," she murmured.

"Are you going to talk to Rafe?"

"Not now. Not yet."

Kerry used the key fob to disengage the car alarm. "Hungry?"

"No. If you could drive me home, that

would be great."

"Are you sure? You know you can stay with me as long as you want."

"I'm sure. I need to sleep in my own bed." She opened the passenger side door.

"I won't get offended, but the offer is good if you change your mind." She opened her door and got in. "What about work? Are you going in tomorrow?"

Avery snapped her seat belt in place. "Have to. I've barely been back and already had to take a day off. I don't need to add to Director Fischer's doubts. He said the promotion is still out there. Hopefully the media interest in me and Rafe has died down — especially since there's nothing to write about," she added and turned her head to stare out of her window. Not to mention that she didn't need her father getting wind of what was going on before she had a chance to tell him herself. It was only a matter of time before he found out. But she needed to steal as much of it as she could for now.

Kerry didn't comment. Avery would work it out. She always did.

After a stop at the pharmacy to pick up her prescription, Kerry dropped Avery home and promised to call later.

■ ■ ■ ■

Sitting in a tub full of bubbles, surrounded by low lights and the unwinding aroma of lavender, Avery leaned back against the lip of the tub and closed her eyes. Steam wafted around her. She missed him. From the depths of her soul she missed him. Her insides twisted and unwound. Rafe was the man she wanted. But what if she would never be well? What if she decided to try to work it out, but he was still in love with Janae? Her heart tightened. She had to be all right. Rafe *had* to choose her. But if she was always going to be a semi-invalid, living on pills and stuck behind a desk or worse, she knew she would be a horror to live with, to love. And she'd grow to resent Rafe and he'd eventually resent her for ruining his life — *again.*

She opened her eyes and stared up at the white ceiling. It was best to let go now.

Rafe's flight landed in New Orleans shortly before six. The travel time between Florida and Louisiana was barely two hours. He wished it was longer. He wished he could stay up in the air, let the clouds separate him from the reality of firm ground for a little while longer.

Seeing Janae shook him more than he was willing to admit. Feelings for her still simmered under the surface. Being with her brought back a tidal wave of memories and raw emotions. But he had to reconcile with the reason why he was facing her for the first time in sixteen years. She'd deceived him.

He got it. He understood why she'd stayed away. In some macabre way she was trying to protect his feelings, and her parents were trying to protect her. But Janae honestly believed that he would have walked away.

That's what unsettled him the most. How could she say that she loved him if she believed that he wouldn't have loved her enough to stay — no matter what? How do you love someone and allow him to believe that you're dead, allow him to wallow in the guilt of loss?

Would he have stayed in Florida and tried to figure it all out without the *possibility* of Avery? The question plagued him as he drove home from the airport. He needed to see Avery, be with her and settle things between them. She was going to listen to reason.

He instructed his phone to dial his aunt Jacquie while he drove.

"Rafe. Sweetie. Are you back?"

"Yeah. Actually, I was hoping you were home."

"Coming by?"

"Yeah. Should be there in about forty minutes."

"I could use the company."

"See you soon."

When Rafe arrived, Jacqueline took one look at his face and wrapped her nephew in her arms. For several moments she held him like she did when he was a wild rambunctious child who had been punished for his antics by his father and sought out his aunt to hear his hurt and grievances.

Reluctantly Jacquie released him, slid her arm around his and ushered him into the house.

"I just turned off the pot."

Rafe grinned. "Smells like a jambalaya party."

"Comfort food. Come on."

Rafe shrugged out of his lightweight brown leather jacket and hung it on the back of the kitchen stool.

Jacquie busied herself at the oven. She took out a tray of rolls and placed them on the marble island counter.

"Hot damn, Aunt J." He snatched a piping-hot, homemade roll from the tray and popped it back and forth between his fingers while he blew on it.

She glanced at him over her shoulder. "If you'd wait a second you wouldn't have to do all that," she said with laughter in her voice.

Rafe blew on the perfectly browned, butter-lathered roll and took a bite. His long lashes lowered over his eyes as he hummed in satisfaction.

She took two large ceramic bowls from the cabinet and set them on the table along with cutlery. Rafe jumped up with his mouth filled with a roll and took the stainless-steel stew pot from the stove and set it on the warming tray in the center of the counter.

"Did Raymond leave yet?"

Jacquie blew out a breath. "This morning. Guess that's why I started cooking." She looked at her nephew. "Comfort."

He patted her hand. "He's gonna be fine, Aunt J."

"I know. It's just hard being sidelined. You know I'm not used to that," she said and puttered a sad laugh.

Since his aunt's near-death diagnosis two years earlier, and her brother Branford being her savior, she'd scaled back on her travel, especially extended travel. Jacqueline

Lawson was a renowned photojournalist whose work was featured in magazines and museums around the world. Her partnership with Raymond only solidified her cache and his. But the doctors wanted her to give her body another six months of high nutrition, rest and follow up, and then she would be one hundred percent back to herself.

Fortunately, she had a husband like Raymond who was strong enough to withstand the Lawson wrath when she fought tooth and nail to go against doctor's orders and chase the next story. He'd put his foot down and let her know that there was nothing out in that world that was more important than what they had together, and they would be nothing without each other. He had no intention of losing her over some job, and if she loved him as much as she claimed, she'd realize the truth in what he said. The lioness purred.

Jacquie ladled heaps of the mouthwatering jambalaya into Rafe's bowl and then hers. She took a seat next to him, waited for him to break the silence.

"She's the same but different," Rafe finally began slowly, and took a spoonful of food. Thoughtfully and at times with difficulty he recounted his meeting with Janae.

Jacquie listened with patience, never

interjecting her thoughts or opinion, only from time to time lovingly patting his hand.

"I've been back and forth in my head," he said on a breath of confusion. "Avery pretty much ended things between us. Janae was willing to start over." His cheeks puffed, he blew out a slow breath, turned and looked at his aunt. "Why are women so difficult?"

Jacquie chuckled. "You askin' the wrong woman if you check with my husband. But, seriously, we're nurturers at heart, always wanting to take care of others, even by sacrificing ourselves in the process." She clasped his fisted hand. "You, Rafe Lawson, bring out that quality in women in spades. They all want to take care of the bad boy, tame his heart, tend to his wounds."

"So, I gotta be a bastard to women? Is that the answer?"

"No, of course not. What I'm saying is you need to be aware that when women love, they protect. Janae was trying to protect you, as hard as that is to digest, and I firmly believe that Avery is trying to protect you from something, as well." She stared directly into his questioning gaze.

"If you're ever going to find some peace inside yourself, whatever you decide to do about Avery, you need to find out what she thinks she's protecting you from. You see the aftermath of how that belief can go terribly wrong," she added.

He focused on the contents of his bowl and churned his aunt's advice over in his head. He turned to her and offered up that heart-stopping half grin. "Plan to."

"Sounds like a toast is in order." She hopped up from her seat, went into the living room and returned with a bottle of bourbon, which she held high like a trophy. She poured for them both.

Rafe lifted his glass. "To the wisest aunt a nephew could have."

Jacquie grinned. "I'll drink to that."

Rafe and Jacquie talked and laughed and ate long into the night. When he woke the following morning, he knew exactly what he had to do. After a long, hot shower and a change of clothes that he kept in his go-bag, he met up with his aunt in the kitchen. She was totally absorbed in the newspaper while she sipped on a cup of espresso.

"Mornin'. Sleep okay?" she asked, looking up as she absently tucked a wayward lock back into the high twists on her head.

"Yeah, I did actually," he said on a breath.

"Coffee?"

"To go. I'm heading out."

She turned halfway on the stool and

looked at him. "Where?"

"DC."

She smiled and then turned back to her paper. "Good. Thermos in the cabinet over the sink," she added, hooking a thumb over her shoulder.

Rafe poured coffee into the thermos and then came up alongside his aunt. "Thank you for listening, Aunt J." He leaned down and kissed her soft cheek.

"And you make sure you do the same," she said, wagging a warning finger.

He winked and walked out. Keeping an open mind was the plan, but he'd seen many of the best laid plans fall apart. He was willing to listen if Avery was willing to talk honestly.

CHAPTER 20

Avery was at her desk, working her way through her mind-numbing assignment of determining which agents were up for new detail assignments. Although the in-house policy was to keep the agents with the same clients, periodically, for a variety of reasons an agent was reassigned. At least she still had her job, such as it was.

She lived for being in the field. She relished the uncertainty, the level of focus needed no matter how mundane an assignment may appear to be. Sitting behind a desk was not what she'd worked and trained for. It was not what the previous director saw in her.

Heaving a sigh, she made a note next to an agent's name when her cell phone began to vibrate on her desk. She snatched it up and the air hitched in her throat. "Hello . . ."

"Hey."

The smooth sound of his voice enveloped

her like a warm blanket. "Rafe."

"I didn't want to be too presumptuous and pop up at your job without calling."

"You're here? In DC?"

"Got in about twenty minutes ago. Still at the airfield. Didn't know if I was going to have to turn right back around. Do I?"

Her heart raced. "No. I . . . want to see you."

"When are you free?"

"I'm off at six."

"I'll come to you around eight. You are back in your place, aren't you?"

"Yes."

"Everything been okay . . . reporters bugging you?"

"No. It's been quiet."

"Good." He paused a moment. "We have a lot to talk about, Avery. Lot to straighten out."

Her stomach clenched. "I know," she said softly.

"I'll see you at eight."

"How long will you be in DC?"

"That depends on how the night goes. I'll see you later."

Rafe picked up his car that he kept parked at the landing strip and drove to his Arlington home for a quick change of clothes before meeting his father for a late lunch.

He'd half expected his very busy father to be unavailable or out of town, but was oddly surprised that not only did he agree to meet with his son, but invited him to lunch at the club where the politicians on the Hill gathered for meals and to cut deals.

As much as he disliked wearing a tie, he'd don one for the occasion, knowing that if he didn't, it would be the first bone of contention on the long list between him and his father. He chose a custom-tailored, slim-fitting charcoal-gray two-piece that he had made at the renowned Martin Greenfield's Clothier during one of his trips to New York. He surveyed the row of shirts hanging in his walk-in closet and finally settled on a pearl-gray shirt. He paired it with an obsidian tie with barely perceptible maroon stripes.

Dressed and as mentally ready as he could be, he took the prenup from his go-bag, stuck it in the inside pocket of his suit and then headed out. He tossed his bag into the trunk of his Benz and headed out of Virginia to DC.

His father made reservations at Charlie Palmer's Steak House on Constitution Avenue. It was his father's favorite place. At any given time an array of who's who could be found huddled over the linen-topped tables, or sequestered in the private dining room. His father always said the service and the food was impeccable and that that was the real reason he went there. But Rafe knew better. The steaks reminded Branford Lawson of home and the atmosphere reeked of the power that Branford Lawson wielded in Washington.

He pulled up in front of Charlie Palmer's and a red-vested valet came to take his car. When he walked inside the tables were filled with suited men and women, waiters were balancing trays of wine and expensive liquor, and crystal flutes and tumblers gleamed beneath the chandelier lighting.

"Reservation?"

He blinked and focused on the young woman in front of him. "Yes. Lawson."

"Oh, yes, the senator is here already. I'll take you to your table."

Rafe walked behind her and spotted a few familiar faces on their way to his father's table — the two hosts from MSNBC, the speaker of the house was holding court in back, and he was pretty sure he spotted the junior senator from New Jersey in an animated conversation with his senior counterpart from New York.

His father had a private table by the window.

"Dad."

Branford lifted his gaze from the sheaf of papers in front of him. "Son." He extended his hand to the seat opposite him. "You look well."

"Thanks." He pulled out a chair and sat.

"I ordered for both of us. Save some time."

Of course he did. He signaled for the waiter. "Bourbon." He linked his long fingers together and focused on his father. "I got the papers from your lawyer."

"Good. The firm is very thorough, made sure you were protected."

"Protected? From what, Dad?"

Branford leaned back in his chair and surveyed his son from above his half-framed glasses. "You never fully understood the vastness of the Lawson fortune."

"Don't you get it? I don't care about all that. I'm building my own fortune, my own legacy."

Branford snorted a laugh just as the waiter arrived with the meals.

"Thank you, Ralph. Looks great as always."

"Of course, Senator."

Branford unfolded a white linen napkin and tucked it in his collar. He pursed his lips. "Food is excellent." He lifted a steak knife toward Rafe. "Eat up."

196

Rafe tossed back his drink and then set the glass down on the table.

Branford cut into his steak and put a piece in his mouth. He chewed slowly. "What this family has, who we are, didn't just happen with your granddad Clive." He rocked his jaw.

"What are you talking about?"

"Your great-grandfather Raford worked the land."

"I know that. He married MaeJean Hughes."

"They were barely more than slaves. Worked for the Fontaines."

"Dad, what does any of this have to do with *you* writing a prenup for *me*?"

"That land that old man Fontaine left to your great grandfather wasn't just any land. It was the seed for everything we have. The land birthed a string of small businesses, employed half the black folks in the area, multiplied and spread." He paused, looked Rafe dead in the eyes. "Son, we own all of St. Mike, Everett, Joe and Montgomery parishes. All the land and businesses running along the south bank of the Mississippi, straight down to the delta."

Rafe listened in stunned silence, trying to absorb the enormity of it all. "Why . . . didn't we ever know this?"

"You're the eldest. The heir. Your uncles know. Grandpa Clive told each of us when we married. The eldest sons are told when they marry." He leveled his gaze at Rafe. "The legal arrangement wasn't meant to control you — no one can do that —" He laughed lightly. "It was to protect our legacy and ensure that it would continue for the next generation. You're the one that everything will fall to. You'll be responsible for the prosperity of the businesses, the lives of employees, homeowners, the rest of the family, your siblings." He leaned forward. "It's why I've been so gotdamned hard on you, son. I needed you to be ready."

"Why didn't you just tell me, Dad? Talk to me."

Branford nodded. "You're right. I should have. When you got engaged to Avery, I knew it was time. This," he waved his hand between himself and Rafe, "isn't my forte. Pretty sure you know that." He turned his attention back to his steak.

Rafe put down his knife and fork. "There's something I need to tell you, too."

"All this time . . ." He stared at his son with astonishment. "Son, I am so sorry."

Rafe nodded.

"What are you going to do?"

198

"There's no going back. That much I know for sure. I'm going to see Avery this evening. Talk. Work it out."

"Make her listen. She's the right woman for you, son."

Rafe angled his head to the side. "Oh, really?"

"I like her."

"Yeah, me, too."

Branford raised his glass. Rafe did the same. The two talked and ate and drank while the lunch crowd disappeared and the early dinner customers arrived. The walls came down. They allowed themselves to be seen in ways they had not in the past, and it felt really good.

By the time they left the steak house, the sun was beginning to take a dip. They stood together in front, while Rafe's car was brought around. Branford's driver pulled up, as well.

"Dad, you had him waiting all this time?"

Branford shrugged. "I had food sent out and told him I'd call when I needed him back."

Rafe chuckled. "You're getting soft in your old age."

Branford grumbled in the back of his throat.

The valet arrived with Rafe's car. He

turned to his father, extended his hand for a shake as they usually did. To his surprise his father pulled him in for an embrace and patted him solidly on the back.

"You work things out with Avery, and we'll talk more about the future."

Rafe's throat tightened. He looked into his father's eyes. "I'll call you."

"I'd like that."

The valet handed Rafe his keys. He gave a final glance at his father, got in the car and drove off.

As he drove home it took all his concentration to focus on the road and the blooming evening traffic. His head was spinning with everything his father revealed to him. The Lawson family was not just well-off. They were beyond wealthy. They wielded the kind of wealth that shaped the landscape, government, altered the narrative, determined outcomes. He drove through large swaths of land, past buildings and homes, and realized for the first time that he was the steward over all of this and more. The magnitude of it was humbling and unsettling as he struggled to wrap his mind around it all. Then of course, there was his own businesses to run.

He pulled into his driveway and went inside. As much as he hated to admit it, the prenup made sense. Although he didn't believe that Avery would ever take advantage, it was to protect her as well as the family.

He tugged on his tie and jogged up the stairs to his bedroom. It was nearly six thirty and he had every intention of getting to Avery's at eight on the dot, and he wanted to stop on the way and pick up a bottle of the wine that she liked.

After a quick shower and change of clothes, he repacked his go-bag with fresh clothes and toiletries, along with the prenup. He exhaled. He seriously hoped that Avery was up to and willing to talk. They had a lot to hash out, but it was going to take a real commitment from them both to make it work. He could only do so much by himself.

CHAPTER 21

Avery checked the time — again. It was ten minutes later than the last time she'd checked. Her stomach was in knots and her heart kept thudding. The last thing she wanted was to get herself worked up and usher in an attack. She looked at the bottle of medicine on her dresser and debated taking a tablet, but decided against it. She needed to be clear and focused and since she had not taken these new meds before, she had no idea how her body would react. She'd debated with herself ever since Rafe's call whether

or not she would tell him everything that was going on with her physically. She understood Kerry's rationale that she should be up-front and honest — that he deserved to know the truth. He'd already endured being the recipient of a lie perpetuated by someone he loved.

Janae. He'd seen her by now. Too many

questions about what happened between them trampled through her head. Images of them together, reunited, taunted her. What if he was coming to tell her . . . ?

The doorbell rang and her entire body jerked in alarm. She drew in a long breath, hoping to slow her racing heart. At the door, she paused for a moment with her hand on the knob, neutralized her expression and then pulled the door open.

"Cher."

The soft single word of endearment was like a love song to her ears. Her soul filled with only the kind of joy that Rafe could bring.

He took a step across the threshold, reached out to her and she found herself enveloped in the strength of his arms. She inhaled deeply, filling her lungs with the renewal of his scent, and listened to the pounding of his heart, and the doubts that plagued her slipped away.

Rafe leaned slightly back. Avery looked up into his eyes an instant before his mouth covered hers. His fingers threaded through the soft tangle of her curls, pulling her into the heat of his kiss.

She sighed into his mouth as he kicked the door closed behind him and in the same motion pinned her against the wall.

The heat of their need for each other fused their bodies together.

"I've missed you crazy," he groaned into her mouth.

She tugged at the hem of his Oxford shirt, pulled it out from the waist of his jeans and slid her fingers up and along his chest before loosening the buckle of his belt.

"Here?" he murmured, and suckled her neck.

"Yes. Yes."

Rafe needed no further invitation. His hands knew all her secret places and found them while incrementally baring her warm skin to his hungry eyes. Her shorts and black panties pooled at her feet and the slight pop freed her breasts from the black bra, and he feasted on them as a man starved.

Avery's moans spiraled while Rafe plied her with hot, wet kisses traveling downward until he was on his knees. She gripped his shoulder and bit down on her lip as his tongue separated her folds and awakened the epicenter of her desire with flicks of his tongue.

Rafe cupped her round behind in his palms and pulled her to him, suckled, kissed, licked her until her inner thighs trembled and her belly fluttered. Gently he drew the swollen bud between his lips and teased, stopped, teased some more. Avery whimpered and dug her nails into his shoulders. Her toes curled as a shiver raced up the back of her legs, spread through her limbs and shook her body with explosive jolts of release.

"Oh, god! Rafe . . ." Her knees weakened as another wave swept through her.

Rafe slowly rose draping her long legs over the bend of his arms. She wrapped them around his waist as he found his way inside her, pushing the air out of her lungs. She gasped as he filled her, moved hard and fast inside her — over and over and over until there was nothing he could do to hold back the jettison that flooded her.

Shaken and breathless they slid to the floor, limbs tangled, bodies wet.

"Up against a wall . . . two feet from my front door," Avery managed to say with breathless laughter ringing in her voice.

Rafe braced his palms on the floor behind him and looked at her through the half slits of his eyes. "A testament to your power ovah me, darlin' . . . which isn't totally satisfied." He rocked inside her and his still stiff erection was unmistakable. "What are we gonna do about this?"

Avery smiled mischievously, pressed her

hands against his chest and pushed him onto his back to straddle him.

"Naughty girl." He cupped her breasts, which overflowed his palms as she rolled her hips and rode them to ecstatic release.

Wrapped in a single light blanket, curled on the couch with soft music in the background Rafe and Avery sipped wine between kisses and light touches.

"We really should eat something," Avery said dreamily. She rested her head on his chest.

"I don't feel like moving. Just want to hold you."

Avery snuggled deeper against him, hummed softly under her breath. She wanted this time to last as long as possible to avoid the hard facts they still needed to deal with.

Rafe stroked her hair away from her face, kissed the top of her head. "It's over," he said quietly.

She lifted her head to look at him. "Janae?"

"Yes."

Her heart thumped.

"How . . . how was it, seeing her again?"

"Hard. Unreal. Sad."

She stroked his chest. "I . . . need you to tell me about it."

Rafe drew in a breath. "I went to her house . . ." He told her in bits and pieces what they'd talked about, her reasons for staying away.

"She still loves you." She hesitated. "Do you still love her?"

Rafe leaned his head back and stared up at the ceiling. "I'll always love her, love what we had, but I'm not in love with her. I know that. And I know that there's nothing in me that wants to go back."

Avery was quiet, taking in what he'd said. She could not imagine the agony that he'd experienced that day and all the days that followed. He'd found a way to piece his life together and found love again — with her. She didn't want to do to him what Janae had done. If they were going to build a life together, it had to be on a foundation of trust.

"I need to tell you something," she began.

"Baby . . ." He angled his body to face her. "You could have told me. You've been dealing with this and we should have been dealing with it together. Don't you get it? I'm in this one hundred percent. All in." He hugged her tighter. "I'm going with you to get the results. End of story." He cupped her cheeks in his hands. "Whatever the deal is we'll handle it together. I need you to hear me on this. No damned job is more important than your health and your life. Nothing is more important to me than you. Period. You got that?"

She nodded. A tear slipped down her cheek.

"No more secrets. I don't need you trying to protect me from the truth. Ever." His aunt's words echoed in his head. He kissed her softly, tasted her tears. "It's going to be all right, baby." He brushed the damp tracks on her cheeks away with his thumb.

She sniffed.

He sat up. "Now I'm starved. And we have a lot more to discuss."

"What?"

"Let's order something first and talk over dinner."

CHAPTER 22

They ordered two large pizzas, one with sausage and pepperoni for Rafe and the other with extra cheese and broccoli for Avery. Each of them were halfway through before they came up for air.

"Guess we were hungry, huh?" Avery giggled over a mouthful of food.

"Hmm. Umm." Rafe washed down his pizza with a long swallow of red wine.

Avery tucked her legs beneath her. "So . . . what else? The suspense is killing me." She leaned back and sipped on her glass of wine.

"It's about the prenup." He watched her expression tense. "I know what you said and how you feel. First of all, I didn't get it written up."

Avery frowned. "You didn't. Then —"

"My father did it. But you didn't give me a chance to explain that part of it."

"Rafe . . . I . . . I'm sorry. I just thought —"

"I get it. I would have figured the same thing, unless you know my father. He likes to have his hand in everything."

"I of all people should understand that. I'm the poster child for the controlling parent." She reached out and touched his cheek. "I'm sorry. I shouldn't have jumped to conclusions." She pushed out a breath. "Honestly, it was just an excuse."

"Huh?"

She took his hands. "This whole being in love and devoted and committed to someone or something other than myself and my career is unchartered territory for me. I got scared. And I stupidly figured that if I found a way out I wouldn't be around to be hurt or . . . to lose you."

"Woman! I'm not gonna hurt you. I'm not leaving and you're not losing me."

"Promise?"

"Yeah." He grinned, but the seductive smile slowly dissolved. "There's more."

Avery set down her glass.

"I went to see my father today. About the prenup."

"Okay."

"He told me the real reason why he had it drawn up."

Her tapered brows drew together. "The real reason? What are you talking about?"

He refilled her empty glass and handed it to her. "Take a sip. You'll need it."

"You're scaring me." She slowly reached for the glass.

"Darlin', scared is putting it mildly."

He got up, crossed the living room to the glass cabinet and took out the bottle of bourbon, poured a short glass and returned to the couch.

Avery's eyes widened in growing alarm. "Rafe . . . what the hell is going on?"

He stood in front of her. "Well . . . you kinda knew that my family was well-off."

"Yes, and?"

"We're a little more than well-off." He tossed back the drink and his eyes squeezed shut as the heated liquid slid down his throat. He sat next to her and began at the beginning with his great grandfather.

Avery listened in numbed silence. The enormity of what he told her stretched the bounds of her comprehension. She tried to envision him as this magnate with near-limitless power and resources at his disposal. She knew power, saw it in action and how it had the ability to make or break a person. Too much power corrupts. The state of the country was a testament to that.

But Rafe was to be her husband, the man she'd spend the rest of her life with. She watched his expression shift from awe to excitement to humility. This was not a man that would let the elixir of power poison who he was.

Rafe looked into Avery's eyes. "The prenup is not set up because of a trust issue or that I'd ever not want you to have whatever was mine. It's to protect you in case anything should happen to me. You would not be responsible for all of the entities in any way."

"First of all, nothing is going to happen to you." She sighed. "I get it. I do. When I saw it I understood what I wanted to understand. Not to mention that I had no idea . . ."

"Yeah, me either."

"So now what?"

"Nothing really changes, at least not yet. I come into my inheritance when I get married. Dad said after the wedding — *and* honeymoon —" he winked "— the learning curve will begin."

"And what about your businesses? The foundation? Your music?"

"About that. I didn't get a chance to tell you." His tone softened. "Before everything kinda blew up with us I'd already begun to put some changes in place, shift the management of things so that I could confidently relocate to DC — for you. I know how important your career is and your career is here."

Her throat clenched. She lowered her head and bit down on her lip. "Oh, Rafe." She looked up, her eyes clouded with tears. "I . . . you are the most amazing man I've ever known." Her gaze combed his face. "To have you love me is the greatest gift and my gift to you is my heart, my soul, my undying love and commitment." She leaned in and kissed him long and slow. "We got this," she said against his mouth.

"That's what I've been trying to tell you, darlin'." He tossed the blanket to the floor.

"So, does this mean I can get my twenty bucks back for the pizza?" she teased as he moved between her thighs.

"Whatever I have," he ground out, easing inside her, "is yours."

"You want me to drive you to work?" Rafe asked while he finished shaving.

Avery came up behind him and slid her arms around his bare waist. "No. Not necessary. You know I like to have access to my own car."

He turned, leaned down and kissed her, leaving shaving cream on the tip of her nose. "Yes, ma'am."

"But I'd love to find you here when I come home." She grinned up at him.

"I might be able to arrange that. I have some business to take care of today. Won't take long, and I need to stop by my place, pick up a few things."

"Good." She whirled away.

"You should hear from the doctor today about the results and when you need to come in, right?"

Avery stopped mid-step. "Yes." She turned back around.

Rafe walked toward her. "It's going to be fine. We got this."

She leaned on him for a moment. "I'm going to be late fooling around with you." She pushed against his chest and walked out into the bedroom. But she couldn't turn her back on the fear that churned in her stomach.

Every time her phone rang, her whole body jerked. This time the call was from Director Fischer, who wanted to see her right away.

"Damn," she muttered when she hung up. She slid her cell phone in her pocket, turned off her computer and locked her office door behind her. A million thoughts ran through her head as the elevator ascended to the executive floor. Had the director gotten

214

wind of her visit to Dr. Ryan? More fallout from photographers? She couldn't see a good outcome to the impromptu request.

The doors slid open and she all but slammed into Mike.

"Richards. How are you?"

"Good. Thanks."

"Congratulations are in order. Maybe we could celebrate over drinks." He stepped onto the elevator and the doors closed before she could respond.

Avery continued down the corridor and stopped at the director's administrative assistant's desk.

"Agent Richards. Go right in. The director is expecting you."

"Thanks." She tugged down on the hem of her dark blue jacket and walked toward the director's office. She tapped lightly on the door.

"Come in."

"Good morning, Director Fischer."

"Agent Richards, please come in and have a seat. I'll get right to it," he began before she barely was in the chair. "I know that you were up for the assistant deputy director, and you would probably do a damned good job at it. In fact I know you would."

Here it comes.

He folded his hands and leaned forward.

"However, something has come up that I believe your skills and experience are a perfect match. An opening in the Joint Terrorist Task Force has opened. As you know, our agency works in partnership with the FBI on this task force."

Avery nodded. "Yes, sir."

"Your name was put forward to fill the position of special agent in charge."

She blinked rapidly. "What?"

Director Fischer offered a rare smile. "The assistant position here at the agency is a good one, granted, but it's really a glorified desk job with perks. That's not where your skills lie. You speak multiple languages, your IQ is off the charts, you're one of our best in the field and your investigative abilities are stellar. Not to mention that you're somewhat of a hero around here."

"Thank you, sir."

"I have to admit I did have some concerns about the incident with the reporters while you were on duty. But everything else about your service to the agency outweighs any reservations I may have had. You're not a paper pusher, Agent Richards. You don't have the temperament to be bogged down in bureaucracy and that's a lot of what that assistant position would be."

"I don't know what to say."

"I'll give you a day, two at the most, to get back to me with a decision. I hope you'll seriously consider it. You'd be the first woman in the position," he added to sweeten the pot.

Avery pushed out a breath and stood. "Thank you, sir." She extended her hand, which he shook. She turned and walked out. Her heart was racing. It took all she had not to do a screaming happy dance down the austere corridors of the agency.

She rushed back to her office and the first call she made was to Rafe. It went to voice mail and she was sure she sounded like a crazy person, but she didn't care. Next she called Kerry, but she was talking so fast that Kerry simply hung up and showed up at Avery's office door moments later.

"What the hell is going on?" she demanded as she burst through the door.

Avery paced as if the rug was on fire. "Sit. Sit." She twirled in a circle. "I just got offered to be special agent in charge with the Joint Terrorist Taskforce," she blurted out.

"Say what?" Kerry leaped up out of her seat.

"Yes!" she screeched and pressed her fist to her mouth. "I just came back from the director's office."

"Avery . . . Oh. My. God. This is major.

Girrrl!" She came over and hugged her tight and then stepped back and squeezed her shoulders. "You are going to take it, aren't you?"

"I don't know. I mean it's going to mean travel, long hours. I'm getting married in four months."

"Wait." She held up her hand. "When did this happen again?"

Avery sat on the edge of her desk. "Rafe came by last night." Her cell phone vibrated on her desk. "One sec." She reached behind her and picked up the phone. "The doctor's office."

"Answer it."

Avery swallowed, pressed the talk icon. "Hello? Yes. Sure. Okay. Thank you." She set the phone down. "The results are back."

"And?"

"He wants me to come in this evening to talk about the findings."

"I'll go with you."

"Thanks, but Rafe insists that he go with me."

"Not a problem. And speaking of Mr. Wonderful, what happened?"

"So much. I don't even know where to start."

"You can start from the good part — the

great makeup sex, and work back from there."

Avery cracked up laughing. "Girl, girl. Humph. No words," she said, her cheeks burning with the memories.

"Since I've been replaced as your wingman, let's meet up for lunch. Catch me up."

"Sounds like a plan."

"One good for you?"

"Yep. Meet up in the lobby."

Kerry turned to leave. "See you then."

Alone the whirlwind events of the morning took their toll. Slowly she sat down, rested her elbows on the desk and her chin on her fist, and tried to process everything. She and Rafe were back on track. She would be marrying one of the wealthiest, most powerful men in the country. She'd just been offered a dream job. And her doctor wanted to see her about the diagnosis that he wouldn't discuss over the phone. That was the hard reality that could negate everything else.

She spun around in her chair only to face the wall. Ironic? She turned back and took up her phone, dialed Rafe. This time he answered.

CHAPTER 23

Rafe held Avery's hand as they listened to the doctor explain Avery's diagnosis.

"What you have is what is called PCS or post-concussion syndrome."

"What is that?" Avery asked. Rafe squeezed her hand.

"Post-concussion syndrome has various symptoms, such as headaches and dizziness that you've experienced. They can last for weeks and sometimes months after the injury that caused the concussion. You display the full array of symptoms — headaches, dizziness, fatigue, irritability, anxiety, insomnia, loss of concentration, ringing in the ears, blurry vision."

"Are you saying this is going to last forever?"

"I know the diagnosis sounds frightening, but the good news is the scans show no damage, no fractures, no clots. In other words, you will be fine. It may take a little while longer. But you will be okay. For some reason that science has yet to figure out, women seem to be more susceptible to PCS than men."

"So, I have to live with it."

The doctor nodded. "There are some schools of thought that believe post-concussion symptoms are related to psychological factors, since the most common symptoms are headaches, dizziness and sleep problems. They're similar to symptoms that people that have been diagnosed with depression, anxiety or post-traumatic stress experience."

"So, I'm crazy on top of everything else?"

"No. Not at all. But you did experience a traumatic event. The main thing now is to manage your stress as much as possible. Get as much rest as you can. Take the medication only when needed. But I'd say in another month or so you should be feeling much better." He opened his desk drawer and took out a card, slid it across the desk.

Avery reached for it. "A psychologist?"

"A suggestion. If you feel that you need to talk to a professional about anything that happened during the explosion."

She drew in a long breath and put the card in her purse.

"Do you have any questions for me?"

"What if I'm not hundred percent in another month?"

"Then I would want to see you again and I'd insist that you see the psychologist, because the problem would not be purely physical."

Avery pursed her lips.

"What can I do?" Rafe asked.

Dr. Ryan smiled. "Make her life as easy as possible and make sure that she doesn't overtax herself. Be supportive."

Rafe looked at Avery and winked. He turned to the doctor. "Not a problem."

"Well, that's it. Any questions that come up later, call me. However, if for any reason the symptoms become worse, increase or the medication does not work, contact the office immediately."

Avery nodded and stood. "Thank you, Dr. Ryan."

"Of course. Take care of yourself."

Rafe shook the doctor's hand. "Thanks."

Rafe had taken an Uber to meet Avery at work since she'd insisted on driving her own car. When he opened the passenger door for her, he half expected her to object, but she slid in without a peep.

"The doctor said a mouthful, baby, but the news was good."

"Eventually good."

"Better than *never* good."

She angled her head toward him and shot him "the look."

He threw up his hands in mock surrender. "Sorry." He turned on the car and put it in gear. "The doc did say irritability was a symptom," he mumbled only to receive a punch in the arm. "He left out violence," he added over his laughter. "Let's go get some dinner."

Avery folded her arms and pretended to pout. "Just keep in mind that I may be a little bit crazy."

"About me, I hope."

Avery groaned. "Baldwin's."

"You read my mind, darlin'."

"That's incredible, sweetheart," Rafe enthused. "You deserve it." He took her hands from across the table and brought them to his lips. His voice lowered to a husky whisper. "Nothing sexier than a badass sister with power and a gun."

Avery's cheeks heated. "So you think I should take it?"

"You're damned right. Why wouldn't you?" He released her and sat back. "What did Kerry say?" he asked, knowing that of course she talked it over with her best friend.

"We had lunch today. She said I should take it and that I'd be a fool if I didn't try to work things out with you."

"I knew I liked her."

She pushed her shrimp scampi around on her plate with her fork. "I'd work crazy hours."

"Me too."

"A lot of travel."

"Me too."

"It could be dangerous at times."

"That's the sexy part." He licked his lips. "Look, I get it. If anyone does I do. We'll make it work."

"When would we ever see each other?" Her brows drew together.

"Don't you know who you're marryin', woman? I can make things happen, be where I need to be, wherever you need me to be."

Her eyes danced lovingly across the smooth sculpture of his face. "Why are you so freaking amazing?"

He feigned confusion, shrugged. "I've been told it was in my DNA, or maybe in all the bourbon I've tossed back over the years," he joked.

"I love you, man," she whispered with a

smile beaming across her mouth.

"Love you right back, darlin'." He picked up a sticky barbecue rib and tore off a piece of sauce-drenched meat. "Eat up, 'cause you're gonna need all your energy."

She tipped her head to the side and looked at him from beneath her long lashes. "And why is that, Mr. Lawson?"

He wiped his hands on the cloth napkin, leaned forward. " 'Cause I fully intend to make crazy love to you until you beg me to stop."

Avery leaned in. "If you know nothing else about me, know that I'm not the begging kind of woman."

That slow simmering grin that set her soul on fire moved across his lush mouth.

"Let the games begin, darlin'."

The month of February, already short, was flying by but Avery and Rafe were pretty much inseparable, making the most of the time they had together. Rafe's time was his own. During the day he worked on his music in his studio at his home in Arlington while Avery went through the rigors of processing and training for her new position. At night they had each other, and Rafe made sure that the only thing Avery had to do at the end of the day was absolutely nothing.

He drove her to work — she'd stopped protesting — and picked her up at night. On most nights they stayed at his place and Alice treated them like high-priced hotel guests. They lounged, they talked, watched old movies, listened to Rafe's compositions, held marathon phone and Skype conversations with his sisters about the plans for the wedding, and made love like crazy.

Rafe turned on the fireplace and he and Avery snuggled under a blanket on the couch with their feet up and munched on an oversize bowl of buttered popcorn. The forecast was for a light dusting of snow and from where they sat, they watched the flakes sparkling like liquid diamonds as they passed through the street lights.

"Do you really have to leave tomorrow?"

"My father has been insisting that I sit down with the lawyers. Go over some things. He has the meeting scheduled for tomorrow afternoon."

She rested her head on his shoulder.

"Dominique really wants you to come on down to 'Nawlins and go over some things in person. Whatever those things are." He scooped up a handful of popcorn. "I can't hold her off much longer. My physical and mental well-being are at stake."

Avery tossed her head back and laughed. "Oh, be a big boy." She patted his thigh. "But seriously, I want to go, but things are too crazy at work right now."

"You can come down and join me this weekend. Fly down on Friday and come back Sunday night. Bring Kerry along for backup."

She chuckled. "She is my maid of honor. Fine. I'll come down on the weekend if Kerry can get away."

"Good. Make it happen. I don't want to be away from you too long." He slid his hand beneath the blanket and played a piano riff along the inside of her thighs. "Both of you can stay at the house. I'll arrange your airfare."

Avery closed her eyes and sighed when his fingers maneuvered around the elastic of her panties.

"I'm going to drop you off in the morning, then head to the strip." He leaned closer and nuzzled her neck. "But I'm going to need an extra special send-off."

She turned into him, looped her arms around his neck. "Whatever you say, baby," she whispered before locking her mouth with his.

CHAPTER 24

Avery dragged herself into the house and shut the door and the exhausting day behind her. It had been non-stop between meetings and hours of training; she'd barely had time to blink. Fortunately, it was the start of the weekend and she could relax. She dropped her laptop bag and purse in the foyer and her keys in the glass bowl that sat on the small circular table near the door. She shrugged out of her white wool coat and scarf, hung them on the coat rack and walked into her empty house.

This would be the first night in weeks that she'd spent alone — without Rafe. The first day in weeks that she'd had to drive herself, going and coming. She laughed. *I'm definitely getting spoiled.*

She headed straight for the kitchen and immediately wished that she'd find Alice busy whipping up one of her fabulous meals. Instead she opened a fridge that boasted a half container of milk, apple juice, leftover Chinese — that was suspect at best — and a bag of spinach. She shut the door and pulled open the drawer where she kept her menus, selected one from the Mexican restaurant that she liked and then went to retrieve her phone from her purse.

When she took out her phone and turned it on for the first time in hours she was shocked to see five missed phone calls, and realized with a groan that she'd been so crazy busy all day that she hadn't had a minute to check her phone. Probably Rafe wanting to let her know he'd arrived and check on her, although he usually texted.

She smiled, tapped in her code and pulled up her phone messages. Her heart began to race. It wasn't Rafe's number. It was a Louisiana exchange. She swiped on the number and listened to the frantic voice on the other end. Desiree. Dominique. Jacquie. "Please call as soon as you get this."

No. She couldn't catch her breath. Her thoughts scrambled in a million directions, none of them good. Her finger trembled as she pressed the call-back icon next to Dominique's name. The phone was answered on the first ring.

"Avery?"

"Yes. What's going on?"

"It's Rafe . . ."

Avery reached behind her for the chair. A flash of heat roared through her. "What is it?"

"He never arrived. He never made it to the meeting. No one has heard from him and . . . he went off radar somewhere over the Potomac."

She was going to be sick. "No. That's not possible. He left this morning. He had a meeting at one. He told me." She could hear her own voice rising in pitch, but couldn't stop it. "He told me!" she screamed.

"Avery, they're searching for him now."

"Oh, God." Tears spilled from her eyes. She held her chest as if that would keep her heart from leaping out.

"Lee Ann, her husband and Dad are there in DC. They want to send a car for you and bring you to Lee Ann's house. The rest of the family is booked on a flight first thing in the morning." Dominique paused. "We're going to find him. You know Rafe." Her voice cracked. "He's too crazy and badass to let anything happen."

Avery sniffed, swiped at her eyes.

"Avery?"

"Yes," she managed.

"A car will be there for you in about an hour. All right?"

"Okay. Yes."

"It's going to be okay, Avery. I know it is."

"It has to."

"See you tomorrow, sis."

For several moments after the call ended, Avery sat frozen in place. She knew she needed to get ready, but she couldn't get her body to react. *Rafe.* Her heart twisted in her chest. The sudden ring of her phone jolted her like a bolt of electricity, snapped her out of her malaise. She snatched up the phone. "Hello!"

"Hey, it's me. Didn't hear —"

Avery broke down.

"Avery. What the hell? What's wrong?"

"Kerry . . . it's Rafe . . . his plane."

"I'm on my way. Ten minutes."

Kerry answered the door for Avery, who hadn't moved from her curled position on the couch since Kerry arrived.

"Hi. I'm Kerry, Avery's friend."

"Preston Graham. Lee Ann's husband."

"Any news," she mouthed.

Preston shook his head no.

Kerry led him into the living room.

Avery drew in a sharp breath when Preston walked in. She rose halfway out of the chair. "Any word?"

"No. I'm sorry. Not yet."

"It's dark and so cold." She blinked back tears.

"We're going to find him. The thing now is for all of us to be together, stay strong and positive."

Avery bobbed her head and finally rose to her feet. "My bag is in the hall." She walked out.

"If it's okay, I'd like to go along with you."

"Not a problem."

"I'll follow."

When they arrived at Lee Ann's home in Silver Spring, Maryland, Lee Ann and Branford were gathered in the family room, along with two men in dark suits who looked very official.

Lee Ann came over to greet her, gathered her in her arms. "It's going to be all right," she hummed in Avery's ear before she released her.

Avery pressed her lips tightly together and nodded. "This is my best friend, Kerry."

"Hi, Kerry. Glad you're here. Come in. We're waiting to hear back from the coast guard."

Avery's stomach churned. "Does anyone have any idea what happened? Did he make a distress call, anything?"

"Aviation recorded a distress call, but it

was garbled and then cut off."

She squeezed her eyes shut.

"Come. Sit." Lee Ann ushered her into the family room.

Branford was getting off the phone. He turned to talk to the two men in hushed tones. They nodded in unison. Branford noticed Avery.

She walked over to him. "Senator Lawson."

"How are you, dear?"

"Terrified," she confessed.

He placed a large comforting hand on her shoulder. "Rafe is a survivor."

Her throat clenched.

"Lee Ann, let's get her a drink."

"We have food in the kitchen," Lee Ann said. "Let's get you both something to eat. It may be a long night." She led them into the kitchen.

The long countertop was lined from end to end with chicken, shrimp, rice, salads. Alice entered from a back room with a stack of plates.

An odd feeling of relief flowed through her. Seeing Alice made the nightmare not seem so real. "Alice."

Alice put down the plates and hurried over to Avery. They hugged tightly. "How are you, sweetheart?"

"I don't even know, Alice. Oh, I'm sorry. This is my friend Kerry."

"I've heard good things about you," Alice said.

"You, too. Good to finally meet you."

"Wish the circumstances were better. Come. Get something to eat. There's tea and coffee."

It was the longest night of her life. She slept in fits and starts, jumping at every sound. At some point she fell into a restless sleep. When she finally woke, for a moment she didn't know where she was and then reality hit her and her pulse raced. She grabbed her robe from the foot of the bed and slipped it on.

The sun was barely visible. The sky was overcast with threatening gray clouds. With gritty eyes and aching bones, she went downstairs, following the sound of the television.

The muffled sound of the television was coming from the den. The door was partially opened. She peeked in and stopped in her tracks. Rafe's father was seated in an oversize Chintz chair. The images on the screen showed the icy Potomac and two coastguard vessels. The announcer was saying the search continued for Rafe Lawson, son of Senator Branford Lawson. Lawson's single-engine Cessna had gone down somewhere over the Potomac. So far, parts of the plane had been found, and the rescue efforts continued for the senator's son.

Avery pressed her fist to her mouth to keep from screaming. But then she heard the soft sobs of Rafe's father and her heart nearly broke in half. She quietly pushed the door open and went to kneel in front of him. She took his hands before he could resist.

"He's going to come home," she said with an assurance that she wasn't sure she felt. "He's tough. You said so yourself. He found a way to survive this. He's coming home." She squeezed his hands between hers. "We have to believe that."

Branford glanced up from their clasped hands and looked into her eyes. "He loves you deeply."

She swallowed over the knot in her throat. "I know."

The sound of voices traveled to them from the front door. His children had arrived. Branford straightened and cleared his throat.

"Our little secret," he intoned, referring to his momentary lapse. "Can't have them thinking the old man is getting soft."

Avery offered a tight-lipped smile of agreement.

Branford took her hand and they walked out to meet the Lawson clan.

"Dad! Avery." Dominique hurried over and hugged them simultaneously, followed by Jacqueline and Justin and Bailey.

"Any news?" Dominique asked, slipping out of her mink coat.

"Nothing yet," Branford said.

"Desiree would have come but the doctor said she's too close to term to fly," Jacqueline said. She focused on Avery. "How are you holding up?"

"One minute at a time."

Alice appeared in the doorway. "Coffee is hot, and I'll get some breakfast started."

The group trouped into the kitchen and found seats at the table and island counter.

"I just don't understand. It's been almost twenty-four hours," Dominique cried. "And all anyone has found is debris." She sniffed hard and wiped her eyes. "That's my brother, dammit. They need to do more! Dad. You have to be able to do something." She blinked rapidly.

"Everything is being done. The coast guard, divers. Helicopters."

Avery's belly knotted.

"It was below freezing last night," Jacqueline said morosely.

" 'Morning, everyone." Kerry shuffled into the kitchen, gave Avery a hug and took a seat at the kitchen table. "Any news?"

Avery shook her head no.

Moments later Lee Ann and Preston joined the assemblage.

Alice brought a pot of coffee and set it on the table, tugged the belt on her robe and turned toward the fridge. She took out eggs, bacon, sausages, green and red peppers and shredded cheese. Soon the kitchen was filled with the comforting aroma of frying maple bacon, sausages and biscuits.

"Anything I can do, Dad?" Justin said, coming over to put his arm around his father's shoulder.

"I'm just glad you're here, son." He reached for the remote and pointed it at the television mounted on the wall but left it on mute.

The local news anchor was in the field where fires ravaged the West Coast, while the scroll at the bottom of the screen noted *the search for the downed plane of Rafe Lawson, son of Senator Lawson, is still underway.*

"It's all over the news," Dominique said and poured a cup of coffee. "Somebody had to see something."

Avery felt trapped in some kind of nightmare that she couldn't wake from. She couldn't reconcile her mind with what was actually happening around her. As she looked from one face to the next it was as if she was witnessing someone else's life, nothing that she was part of. Yet to her horror she was part of it.

This time yesterday she was with Rafe, talking and laughing and making plans. Any minute she expected him to come bursting through the doors, taking up all the energy in the room and telling them some crazy story about what had happened.

Lee Ann's voice of assurance pierced her fog.

"Rafe is tough. He's been through his share of near misses. He'll come through this one," Lee Ann insisted and rested her head on her husband's shoulders.

Alice put a platter of bacon and sausage on the table, followed by an enormous tray loaded with a fluffy western omelet. Justin pulled up the rear and set the biscuits on the table.

Avery dared to lift her eyes to the television screen. Her heart leapt at the words emblazoned on the screen: *Breaking News.* "Please turn it up! Turn it up!" She pointed frantically toward the screen.

Dominique snatched the remote and

bumped up the volume at the same time that Branford's cell rang and his security darted into the kitchen holding up a phone. In the background the reporter was saying, "Search and rescue has located Rafe Lawson, found clinging to the rocks. He is being rushed to Georgetown University Hospital. His condition is unknown at this time . . ."

"Oh, my God," Avery screamed.

Branford waved his security over while answering his phone. "Yes. Yes. Thank you. Right away." When he looked up at the wide-eyes of expectation from his family it appeared that ten years had been shaved off his face. "They found him." His voice shuddered with emotion. "He's alive, but unconscious." He took the secured phone from his agent. "Yes, we just heard," he said to the caller. "Heading to the hospital now. Thank you."

Avery trembled with relief as hugs and tears were shared all around. Branford held her the longest.

"Go, all of ya!" Alice instructed. "I'll pack this up."

Everyone heeded Alice's directive and darted off to get dressed.

CHAPTER 25

Nearly two hours later the head nurse came in to advise them that Rafe had been moved to ICU. However, only one person could visit at a time and only for ten minutes.

"I know if it was me in there," Justin said, looking from one to the other, "not that I don't love ya'll but I'd want to see Bailey." He put his arm around her shoulder and kissed the top of her head.

"He's right," Dominique conceded. "You should be the one to go, Avery."

Avery pushed to her feet. "Are you sure?" She looked to Branford and he gave her his blessing with a nod of his head. Avery exhaled, offered a tight-lipped smile to the family and followed the nurse out.

"I don't want you to get upset when you see him," the nurse said as they entered the corridor leading to the ICU. "There are tubes and machines and he's pretty banged up."

She pushed through the swinging doors and it was as if they'd entered a whole other world — something out of a sci-fi movie. Large monitors were mounted strategically throughout. The main nursing station sat in the center manned by four nurses, all in front of computer screens that monitored every patient in the wing.

Behind every glassed room, they passed patients connected to some kind of machine, who appeared ghost-like beneath the white sheets. The only indication of life was the hiss of breathing machines and the eerie beeping like an alien pulse that vibrated through her.

The nurse stopped in front of room 807. "Ten minutes," she said before turning away.

Avery gathered a cloak of strength around her and gingerly approached. She'd seen plenty of bed-ridden patients, some like her mother, sustained only because of machines. This was different. This was her love.

Slowly she approached the bed. The nurse was right. The sight of Rafe, bandaged and bruised, connected to wires and tubes, broke her heart. She heard her own whimpers mix with the hum and beep of the machines.

She pulled up a chair and sat next to him,

took his hand in hers. "Baby, I'm here," she whispered. "The whole family is down the hall, waiting to see you." She stroked his hand. "We were so scared. I . . . don't know what I would do if I lost you, not after all that we've been through. You're going to get better, baby. You have a wedding to attend." She wiped tears from her eyes, glanced at the machine that tracked his heart and pulse. "We have plans, and I can't do them without you. You promised me forever, and I'm holding you to it." She sniffed, leaned over the bedrail and kissed his hand. "Come back to me," she whispered. "If you can hear me, come back to me. I love you so much."

A nurse came in to change the bag of warm saline. "I'm sorry but you're going to have to leave now," she said softly. She hung the new bag and checked the tubes.

Avery nodded numbly and slowly stood and then leaned over and whispered to him, "I'll be back as soon as they let me. Rest. Heal." She kissed his bruised cheek. "Love you, darlin'," she said using his term of endearment.

Throughout the day, the family took turns visiting with Rafe. The doctor advised them that his temperature had returned to normal, his vitals were strong and all they could do now was wait until he woke up.

Avery was sitting next to the bed the following morning, talking softly to him about the new job and all the training she had to go through when suddenly his fingers moved. She jumped up. "Rafe. Rafe. Can you hear me, baby?"

His eyes fluttered open. It took several moments before he was able to focus on Avery. "Who's Rafe?" he asked in a hoarse whisper.

Oh, God, no. Avery's hand flew to her mouth, and then that slow simmering smile moved across his. "Hey, darlin'."

Her heart thundered so fast she could hardly catch her breath. "You! How could you do that?" she screamed, more elated than upset. "Rafe. Oh, baby." She leaned over to hug him and he winced. "Sorry. Sorry. Nurse!"

The nurse came running in.

"He's awake!"

She came around to the side of the bed, took his pulse, checked his pupils and the readings on the monitors. "I'll get the doctor. Welcome back, Mr. Lawson."

CHAPTER 26

"Do you remember what happened?" Avery
asked while he wolfed down a cheese steak
she'd brought him. Great hospital, he'd
said, but the food was lousy.

"Most of it. One minute I was in the air
and the next . . ." He shuddered. "They just
came out of nowhere. A swarm of damned
birds. Knocked out the engine. I lost control." His jaw clenched as the images and
the fear that engulfed him that night filled
his mind. "You know how they say your life
flashes before your eyes?" He snorted a
laugh. "It's true." He turned to Avery. "All I
could think about as that plane was going
down was you — all the times we were
together, the love we made, the promises,
our wedding. I didn't want you to see me in
pieces."

"Babe . . ."

"When the plane hit the water . . ."

Avery squeezed her eyes shut.

"I blacked out I guess," he said slowly as if searching for the words. "When I came to it was freezing. I was so fucking cold." He threw his head back. "It was pitch dark." He frowned, tried to concentrate. "I must have been thrown clear. I don't even know. I found a piece of debris and clung to it. The next thing I remember was waking up in the hospital and seeing you." Janae's words flitted through his head. She'd told him that he was the only constant in her life, the one thing she clung to, the memory. Now he understood, because he'd lived his own version.

"I heard you talking to me."

Avery blinked back tears and held his hand. "You did?"

"I swore I heard you. It was like you were pulling me up out of the water, out of the dark. I knew I had to get to you. Let you know it was gonna be all right."

"It will be. It is," she said and leaned in to kiss him long and sweet. She moved back and stroked his forehead. "Might leave a scar." She lightly ran her finger along the butterfly bandage over his left brow. "Gives you a rugged look," she teased.

"As soon as I can, I'm going to show you rugged, darlin', believe that." He reached up, cupped the back of her head and drew her in for the kiss he wanted. Just to make his point.

"Get a room."

They turned to see Quinten in the doorway, chuckling.

"We already have a room, bro. Folks just won't leave us alone," he joked.

Quinten came in and gave Avery a warm hug. "How you doing, lady?"

She grinned as if she'd won the lottery and shot Rafe a quick look. "Doing real good. Listen, fellas, I'll leave you two alone. I have a few errands to run." She leaned over and kissed Rafe. "See you later, baby."

Avery walked out, warmed by the sound of their laughter. She couldn't wait to get him home. They'd have to devise some innovative techniques until he was completely healed, and she couldn't wait to start experimenting.

The press was camped outside of the hospital the day that Rafe was released more than a week after he was brought in. Lee Ann had suggested that it would be best if Rafe gave a statement to the media, suggesting that it would slow the feeding frenzy and then he could recuperate in peace.

Rafe talked it over again with Avery while she helped him get into his shirt.

"Whatever you need to do," she'd said. "This is Lee Ann's arena down here. If she thinks it's the right move I would take her suggestion."

He winced, held his side and slowly sat down on the one chair in the room.

"You okay?"

"Yeah, yeah. Gonna take a minute."

She got his sneakers from the closet and put them on his feet. "Not much that can be done for cracked ribs. Rest."

"Funny how things happen."

"What do you mean?"

"Couple of weeks ago I loosened the reins on all of my businesses. Now it's good that I did. Got all the right people in place and I don't have to worry about it while I recuperate."

Avery leaned to the side and put her hand on her hip. "I really would have preferred that you found some other way to make space between you and your businesses. Next time you want to make major changes in your life give me a heads up."

"Yes, ma'am."

The nurse arrived with a wheelchair.

"Your chariot, Mr. Lawson," Avery teased. "The family is downstairs."

Avery walked alongside the nurse's aide who pushed the chair down the hall. She bent down to whisper in his ear. "Be your sexy, charming self so I can get you home — alone."

"Naughty girl. I'll talk fast."

Lee Ann, Dominique, Justin and their father met Rafe and Avery in the lobby of the hospital.

"The car is right out front," Lee Ann said. "Plenty of reporters out there. You have a feel for these things," she said, pressing his shoulder. "Say as much or as little as you want."

He glanced up with a lopsided grin. "I got this, sis. Not my first rodeo with these folks."

"Don't we know it," Dominique quipped.

"Very funny," Rafe responded. "Okay, let's do this."

Branford opened the glass exit doors and Justin took over for the nurse, pushed the wheelchair down the ramp and the media descended.

Immediately Avery's protective instincts and training kicked in. Her first reaction was to block him from the crowd that approached and scope out any potential threats, anyone out of place who didn't look right. There was the general array of print and television media, many faces that she recognized from her various details, and of course there were the curious bystanders

248

who stopped to see what was going on. Her gaze continued to scan the crowd while keeping within inches of Rafe.

Slowly he rose to his feet. Avery watched him contain the pain as he came to his full six-foot-three-inch height. He still sported the bandage over his eye and his thigh was thickly bandaged under his gray sweats, his ribs taped beneath his Tulane University hoodie, and Avery couldn't describe how utterly edible he was.

"How are you feeling, Mr. Lawson?" one reporter shouted.

"Like I'm getting over being in a plane crash," he said with his patent roguish smile.

The crowd chuckled.

Rafe held up his hand. "But seriously. I'm very lucky to be here. My family, the coast-guard team never stopped looking for me. I had the best doctors here at Georgetown who patched me up — pretty much brought me back from the dead. And I want to thank everyone involved."

"Planning on getting up in a plane again?" another reporter called out.

"Soon as I can." He started to sit back down and Justin grabbed his arm to help.

"Senator Lawson! Senator Lawson, any comment about your son's miraculous rescue?"

"I'm very grateful, and I think my son has said the rest. Thank you all very much." He walked ahead and got into his Suburban.

"Senator Lawson, do you think that you being the chairman of the Homeland Security Committee had anything to do with your son's plane crash?"

Branford stopped halfway in and halfway out of the door of the Suburban. He turned toward the reporter. "Unless terrorists can command bird strikes I doubt it very seriously." He shook his head in annoyance and got in the car.

"How does your fiancée feel about you wanting to fly again?" another reporter tossed out to Rafe.

Avery inwardly flinched, second-guessing her decision to be present. The last thing she needed was to get tossed back under the spotlight.

"Ya'll know I'm a true Southern gentleman and one who never tells. Thanks, ya'll." He sat down, and Justin pushed the wheelchair toward the waiting SUV.

Avery bit back her smile. He was right. He knew how to handle the media like a pro. The whole family did.

As Rafe was wheeled past the phalanx he caught a flash in his peripheral vision. "Wait." He suddenly gripped Justin's hand.

"What's wrong?"

Avery stopped short, as well. "What is it?"

Rafe looked again. His gaze raced over the crowd. "Nothing." He frowned. "Sorry. Thought I saw someone. Let's go."

Avery studied the faces and the bodies of the dispersing crowd, while Justin helped Rafe into the SUV. Something spooked him. But what? She waited until everyone was in the SUV before she got in, taking one last look before shutting the door.

Branford returned to the Capitol. Lee Ann, Dominique and Justin came by Rafe's home, made sure he was settled and then went back with Lee Ann to her home in Silver Spring. Dominique, Justin and Bailey were booked on flights to leave in the morning. Jacqueline would return to New Orleans at the end of the week and promised to help Alice out during the day while Avery was at work.

"Alone at last," Rafe said and stretched his arm out for Avery.

She eased down next to him on the couch and gently adjusted the pillow under his elevated leg. "Need anything?" She pressed her palm to his chest.

"Just you." He brushed his thumb across

251

her bottom lip, turned as much as his cracked ribs would allow and leaned in to kiss her.

Avery melted against him, physically needing him with a ferocity that swirled with hurricane force inside her. She moaned into his mouth as the tip of his tongue pressed and danced with hers. A match of desire lit in her belly, the warmth spread to her limbs, intensifying when Rafe slid his hand beneath her blouse. As much as she wanted to feel him inside her, she knew for the time being that second base was as far as they could go.

"Get undressed," he ground out and then sucked on her bottom lip with his teeth.

Avery's lids fluttered open. She reared her head slightly to look him in the eyes. "Rafe . . . we can't . . ."

"Get undressed," he said again. "I need to see you."

She drew in a shaky breath and slowly stood in front of him.

Rafe rested his head against the cushion of the couch and watched, with growing lust, the show unfolding in front of him.

Avery unbuttoned her starched white blouse and let it fall to the floor. She reached behind her and unfastened her black lace bra, slid one and then the other strap off her shoulders and tossed it aside. Rafe's eyes darkened. A groan rumbled in his chest. "Keep going."

There was only one time she'd ever felt shy and uncertain with Rafe, and that was during the very first time they'd made love. But he'd made her feel not only beautiful and desirable but invincible. She knew that however she felt, weak or strong she could be those things with him and it would be okay. This moment was different. She felt like she was readying herself to be with him for the very first time.

"Everything," he insisted.

Her fingers trembled ever so slightly as she unzipped her slacks and slid them down. She stepped out of them and repeated the act with her panties. She'd never felt more vulnerable in her life. But when she witnessed the look of love, admiration and heat in his eyes, her insecure moment evaporated.

"You're so beautiful," he whispered.

Her entire body heated. She stroked her lip with her tongue.

"Come here."

She took the few steps, but he stopped her when she was close enough to reach out and touch. He languidly caressed her hip, her thighs.

"Put your foot up here." He patted the space on the couch next to him.

Her breathing escalated. Rafe stroked the inside of her thighs until she began to moan. His fingers teased her slit, which grew slippery and wet with an invitation that he willingly accepted. She gripped the back of the couch to steady herself and gasped when his finger slid inside her.

"Closer," he urged.

Her head spun.

"Closer," he said again, and then his mouth was on her, his tongue in her.

"Ahhhh!" Her fingers dug into the couch. She cupped the back of his head and gave herself over to him.

His mouth was magic, casting an erotic spell that she wished would last forever. His tongue flicked and teased and licked until she was weak. The pit of her stomach fluttered. She heard her cries rise above her pounding heart as the first wave of release whipped through her. Rafe gripped her rear and squeezed in rhythm with the pulse that throbbed within her wet walls until she was spent.

She slipped down onto the couch, mindful of not tumbling on Rafe while she pulled herself back from the heavenly ride he'd taken her on. She rested her head on his chest and closed her eyes. What they'd just done played behind her lids. An unbidden moan slipped from between her lips.

Rafe twisted a lock of her hair around his finger. "You good, cher?"

"Hmm, umm," she murmured. Her hand drifted down his chest past his bandaged ribs and inched beneath the elastic waistband of his sweats until she wrapped her hand around his thickening erection.

He sucked in air through his teeth. "Naughty girl."

"Returning the favor . . ."

CHAPTER 27

Rafe's eyes fluttered closed and then opened halfway. "I think you took advantage of me in my weakened state."

"I'd have to say that you rose to the occasion. Pun intended."

He winced from the pain when he laughed.

"You want to take a pill?"

He shook his head no as he settled in bed. "I'll ride it out. Not too bad."

"What about your leg? Coming up the stairs . . ."

"Nothing I can't handle, darlin'."

She leaned over and kissed him. "I'm going to let you get some rest." She adjusted the pillows and pulled up the comforter. "Alice fixed a bunch of food. I'm going to see what I can heat up."

He yawned. "Sounds good." His eyes drifted close. "Nurse . . . maybe you could give me a sponge bath later."

Avery burst out laughing. "You are terrible. Get some rest." She turned out the light next to the bed and tiptoed out.

When she checked the double-door fridge, she had no idea one woman could cook so much food. Every shelf was stacked with food — rice dishes, potato salads, fried chicken, rice and beans, crawfish, steamed vegetables, shrimp and even a large container of lobster bisque. She shook her head in astonishment. Every plastic container was labeled. "This woman needs to open a business." She took out a container of shrimp and one of red beans and rice. She took down a plate from the cabinet, spooned on food from the containers and then popped the plate in the microwave. She had a pretty good feeling that Rafe was fast asleep, but she was starving.

While she waited for the food to heat, she turned on the television. The local news was on. She was going to surf past it to MSNBC when the familiar backdrop of George Washington University Hospital filled the screen and the Lawson family leaving the hospital.

"Earlier today, flanked by family and security, Rafe Lawson, son of Senator Branford Lawson, was released from GW Hospital after more than two weeks, following a

257

near-fatal plane crash. The younger Lawson has built a reputation on his daredevil lifestyle and his array of beautiful women. Most recently he's been paired up with Senator Horace Richards's daughter, Avery Richards, with a wedding date set for late spring. When asked today what his fiancée had to say about him flying again, this was his response . . ."

They played the clip of Rafe's very gallant response.

Avery smiled. He was born to be a star. The camera loved him. A real natural. Then suddenly his open, engaging expression tensed, as if he'd seen a ghost. She looked closer. That was the moment he'd stopped the wheelchair. He saw something in the crowd. She only assumed it then but she knew for certain now.

The microwave dinged.

Commercial.

Avery stood over the bed, watched him sleep. She should leave it alone. He said it was nothing, but her antenna pinged, and she wouldn't rest until she knew for sure. She turned away and went to take a shower before turning in for the night. In the morning. They'd talk in the morning.

258

Something woke her. She blinked into the darkness, tried to pinpoint what had crept into her sleep. She reached for Rafe, and the space beside her was empty. She sat up, peered into the darkness and made out his figure sitting in the chair by the window. The full moon cast him in a forlorn halo.

"Rafe?" She tossed the covers aside and got out of bed and padded over to where he sat. "You okay?" She caressed his cheek and sat on the arm of the chair.

"Yeah. A little restless. Didn't want to wake you."

"Can I get you anything?"

"I am kind of hungry. Fell asleep before dinner."

"You needed the rest." She stood. "I'll heat up something."

"Nothing too heavy."

"How about a bowl of lobster bisque and a small salad?"

"Lobster bisque! Don't tell me Alice fixed her secret weapon?"

Avery chuckled. "A tall container full."

"You have *got* to have some."

She stood. "Maybe I will. Be back in a minute."

What he told Avery was only partially true. He was restless, but it wasn't because of pain. It was because he couldn't shake the notion that he'd seen Janae in the crowd. Only an instant, like mist. You know it's there but can't really see it. Maybe it was his imagination and the drugs they'd given him that had him seeing things, but his gut told him differently. What would she be doing here?

He shifted in the chair and slowly lifted his injured leg to rest it on the footstool. Coming to terms about Janae was the most difficult thing he'd ever done. Walking away after seeing her, hearing what happened to her and all that she'd endured, tore him up inside. From the moment he walked out the door he'd questioned — off and on — his resolve to not look back.

"Mind if I turn on the lights?"

He pulled away from the turn of his thoughts. "No. Go ahead. Hmm, smells good."

Avery walked over and gingerly set the tray down on the small square table.

"Looking mighty good in that little pink nighty," he teased and ran his fingers along her bare thigh.

"Bet you say that to all the girls." She sat in the opposite chair and reached for the bowl of soup. "Now let's see what makes this legendary."

"I need to tell you something."

Avery stopped the spoon halfway to her mouth. "Okay." She took a spoonful, and her eyes closed in bliss. "Oh. My. Goodness. This . . . this is . . ." She took another mouthful. "Heaven."

Rafe grinned. "Yeah, told ya."

She set down her spoon with a soft click against the white porcelain bowl, focused on his distracted expression. "What's wrong? What do you have to tell me?"

Rafe looked right into her eyes. "This will sound crazy, but today when we were leaving the hospital, I swore I saw Janae."

Her nostrils flared. "Janae? That's . . . why would she be here? You said she was in Florida."

"She is. I don't know." He shook his head. "It was only a couple of seconds and when I looked again she was gone."

That was it. He *had* seen something or thought he had. She didn't know what to think or how to feel. She gripped the arms of the chair. "Tell me honestly, are you really over Janae?" He started to speak but she held up her hand to stop him. "I'm not accusing or . . . whatever. I just need you to be as painfully honest with me and yourself. What the two of you had and how it ended or didn't changed your life, your heart, and then to find out that she's still alive . . . well it's not something that you simply 'get over.' I wanted to believe that you could. I needed to believe it. But that's not reality. The fact that you think you saw her in a crowd after your own near-death trauma says volumes."

Rafe hung his head. "You're my psychiatrist now?"

"What!"

"Forget it." He slowly lowered his leg to the floor. "I love you. I *loved* her. I won't deny that. I can't. But she was *then.* You are *now.* The fact that I think I might have seen her in the crowd doesn't mean that I have some sort of distorted fantasy about me and her reuniting. Or that we're bound in some kind of way because of what happened to each of us."

Avery pursed her lips. Why was she still so afraid? He'd proved his love for her time and again. He'd loosened the reins on his business so that he could relocate to DC for her. He'd come back to her even after she'd accused him of thinking she was a gold digger. He didn't run when she was terrified of her own health; instead he simply said they were in it together. Time and again he'd confirmed his love for her. So why?

She linked her fingers together. "I've never had a love like this," she said slowly. "I know I've said it all before, and I thought that I was finally finding that space in here," she pointed to her chest, "to simply accept that I'm capable of being loved the way you love me."

"Avery, darlin', you're the toughest, most intelligent, determined woman that I know *when* it comes to your career. You would move mountains for your job. Actually risk your life for your job. But when it comes to us — me and you — the slightest thing and you're ready to jump ship."

"Rafe, I —"

"No. I need you to listen. It took me sixteen damned years to even take a chance on falling for anyone. Anyone. Sure, there've been women in my life. I admit that. But none of them got beyond the walls I'd built — until you. When I met you, Avery, I knew I wanted to try again. But it seems like the harder I try, woman, the harder you push back. Maybe it's all the fucking years of second- and triple-guessing people, always on high alert, waiting for the shoe to fall, to uncover the bad guy that has you in a place where you can't trust." His eyes roamed over her face. "Everyone is suspect — even me."

She drew in fluttering breaths. "You're not — please don't believe that."

He limped to his feet, wobbled for a moment and then steadied himself. "It's not me that shouldn't believe it, darlin'. It's you." He stood over her. "If we're going to make this work you're going to have to trust me and trust yourself. Trust that what we have is real and that the boogeyman is not behind door number two."

Avery slowly stood. She cupped his face in her hands and he slid his arms around her waist. "Please be patient with me." She kissed him. "You had sixteen years and multiple trial and errors to get where you are now."

He started to respond but decided against it.

"I promise it won't take me sixteen years."

His lips flickered with the beginnings of a smile. "You sure about that?" He pulled her close.

"I'm not sure about anything." Her eyes caressed his face. "But when I'm with you, I believe anything is possible."

"That's all I need," he said, lowering his head.

"Oh really?" she cooed and raised her mouth to meet his. "You sure that's all you need?" She brushed her lips across his.

Rafe palmed her rear and pulled her tight against him. "Far from it. Anything you can do about that?"

"I'm pretty sure I can . . ."

CHAPTER 28

"I don't know, Q. Some days I figure it's gonna be all good, and the next I'm not so sure." Rafe absently ran his finger across the small scar over his eye. He picked up his mug of coffee and put the phone on speaker.

"I hear ya, bruh. Look, if anyone knows what you're dealing with, it's me."

Rafe could kick himself for being such an insensitive prick. Quinten not only lost his twin sister, Laci, to gun violence, he lost Nikita, the first true love of his life, in a tragic car accident. No one was sure if he would ever come back from that. He'd given up on everyone and everything and then one day he met Rae. He and Quinten had bonded years ago, but their bond was strengthened by the experiences that they shared. Yeah, Quinten did know.

"Do you still think about her?"

"Nikita?"

"Yeah."

"All the time. Not the same way or with the same pain, but yeah I think about her."

Rafe was quiet. He slowly turned the mug on the counter.

"You're not being disloyal to Avery to think about or even still have feelings for Janae," Quinten said, filling in the space and the unasked question.

"How do you balance the two, make it work?"

"Man, you know I was beyond f'd up after Nikita. But Rae helped me get better. I let myself go with how I felt instead of trying to fight it. Wasn't easy. You, my brother, have a very rare circumstance."

"Yeah, for real."

"Doesn't mean you can't move past it. I'm pretty sure part of what's spooking Avery is Janae literally coming back from the dead. It's one thing to fight off a ghost, but flesh and blood is a whole other story. Look at it from her perspective. And you gotta remember that less than six months ago she was nearly killed, and then your plane crash. I'd be spooked, too."

"When did you get so insightful?" he teased.

"Man, while you was busy running the streets and dating supermodels and whatnot

I was being domesticated. Tapped into my 'feminine' side."

Rafe burst out laughing and Quinten joined in.

"But on the real. We lucky, bruh."

"Lucky?"

"Yeah, both of us got a serious second chance."

Rafe sipped his coffee. "Yeah, we did."

"So like she asked you, give her a chance and give yourself one, too."

"Thanks, man."

"Not a problem. My bill is in the mail."

"Along with my check," Rafe said laughing.

"On another note, how you feeling?"

"Day by day. Ribs are still sore. They took the staples out of my thigh yesterday. At least I can get in the shower now."

"I know that's a relief. Hey, I'm working on some new stuff. I'll send it to you. See what you think."

"Cool. I need to get back to my music. Going stir crazy."

Quinten laughed. "Anyway, bruh, like I said, give Avery a chance. And give yourself one, too."

"That's the plan."

"Later, man."

"Later. Give my love to Rae."

"Will do."

Rafe turned the speaker off the phone.

Alice poked her head in the door. "Going to run some errands. Need anything while I'm out?"

"No. Thanks. I'm good."

"Okay. See you in an hour or so."

Now that he had the house to himself, he decided to take a long, hot bath to get some of the kinks out, and then grub on one of Alice's magic containers and head to his studio. Maybe he'd compose something for Avery and surprise her when she got in from work.

Garbed in his favorite pair of grey sweats, with a bowl of homemade chicken soup in his hands, he headed to his studio.

His in-home studio was modeled after the major recording studios. The soundboard was state-of-the-art and the soundproof plexiglass-enclosed recording space came equipped with standing mics, a keyboard, a drum set and a six-foot couch to crash on.

Playing the keyboard was not his strength, but he knew his way around enough to write his melodies. He'd been playing with some lyrics in his head that he needed to get down on paper. He grabbed a notebook and pencil from the shelf, stretched out on the couch and started to write.

He got up, sat at the keyboard and began teasing out a melody.

Suddenly Alice appeared and tapped on the glass. Rafe waved her in.

"Good to see you in here again."

Rafe grinned. "Feels good. Didn't realize how much I missed it."

Alice stood in the doorway, folding and unfolding her hands. Finally, Rafe looked up.

"Something wrong?"

Her expression tightened and loosened. "I don't know how to say this — I swear I just saw Janae."

The pencil slipped out of his hand. He sat up straighter. "What?"

"It's crazy. I know. But when I was coming up the street there was a car on the corner at the red light. As I was passing the car she turned and looked at me. I was so stunned that I couldn't react. The light changed and she drove off." Alice shook her head. "But it couldn't be Janae." She gave a little shiver.

He thought back to the day he was discharged from the hospital. Her face appeared in the crowd and was gone.

"Oh, I'm so sorry. I didn't mean to upset you. I know all that you —"

"Sit down, Alice. Please."

Hesitantly she slowly lowered herself onto the end of the couch.

"Something you need to know. Probably should have told you sooner."

"Told me what?"

"Janae isn't dead."

"Oh, my God." Her hand flew to her chest. "I don't . . . what are you saying?"

"Aunt Jacquie got a call . . ."

Rafe unfolded the story for Alice, who sat in opened-mouth silence, an expression of utter disbelief etched on her almond-brown face.

"I don't know what to say or what to feel. All these years," she said, the sound of awe mixed with sadness laced in her voice. "Are you okay?"

"Getting there. I mean it rocked me. I won't lie."

"You said you think you saw her at the hospital and now she's at the house."

"Pretty sure if that was her that you saw, then it was her that rang the bell a few minutes earlier. I ignored it."

"Rafe, I don't like the sound of this. How did she know where you lived? You bought this place after —"

He pushed out a breath. "I don't know. But there isn't much you can't find out on the internet. For all I know she may have followed the car home from the hospital."

"That was weeks ago. She's been here in Virginia all this time?"

"Apparently."

"I don't like this. Did she seem . . . okay when you saw her in Florida?"

"I guess. I mean I think I was so rocked by seeing her again I didn't focus in on anything that could be wrong." *I still love you, Rafe.* "The last place I expected her to be is here."

"Avery knows?"

He nodded.

"Maybe you should call her, Rafe. If it really is her, then you need to find out what it is that she wants."

Rafe stared off into the distance. "I'll think about it."

CHAPTER 29

"How's everything going with the new position?" Rafe asked while he washed Avery's back.

She lifted her face up to the shower and then turned toward him. "Getting the feel of things. It's different. A lot more responsibility, learning the culture of the department, new personalities. But it's good."

"Hmm."

She brushed her wet hair away from her face and studied his closed expression. "Something wrong? You've been weird all evening."

He blinked and focused on her. "I'm good. Just thinking about this piece I was working on today."

Her brows shot up. "You were in the studio?"

He bathed in her enthusiasm. "Yeah."

"And?"

"Got started on a piece. Still some more

work to do." He reached around her and turned off the faucets.

"Can't wait to hear it." She grabbed a towel from the rack, handed it to him, took one for herself and then another to wrap her hair in.

"Soon as I'm done." He kissed her forehead. "Promise." He tucked the towel around his waist and strode into the bedroom.

"We haven't talked much about your health since you started the new job."

Avery curled closer to Rafe and pulled the sheet up over her shoulder. "Wow, now that I'm actually thinking about it — I haven't had an attack in weeks."

"Really, nothing at all?"

"No." The excitement rose in her voice. She rose up halfway. "Pain free. I haven't had to take any medication. With all that went on with you," she draped her leg across his, "and the new job I hadn't even noticed."

Rafe kissed her forehead. "Aw, darlin'."

"The doctor did say it would take a while."

"Yeah, so that doesn't mean to go buck wild because you're feeling good." He chuckled.

She playfully swatted his chest. "Guess everything happens in its own time. And speaking of things in their own time, we never did get to go to New Orleans."

"Hmm, true. I'm free as a bird." He laughed. "We have to work around your schedule."

"Could we do a weekend?"

"Whatever works."

"And we're going to fly in a regular plane, like regular people."

"Yes, ma'am."

She ran her hand gently along his chest. "Better?"

"Almost good as new. Just a twinge every now and then." He turned toward her and ran his hand along her bare side. "Maybe we should test it out." His mouth pressed against hers and his tongue teased her lips before dipping inside her mouth.

She shifted her body beneath him.

"Love you, cher," he whispered.

She stroked his cheek and parted her thighs for him. "Show me."

He made a noise deep in his throat. "With pleasure."

Alice usually arrived around eleven and Avery was gone by eight. He paced the bedroom, debating while he turned the phone over and over in his hand. He had to know for sure. He tapped in his password, swiped for his contacts until he reached her name.

The phone rang and rang on the other end until the voice mail kicked in.

"Janae, this is Rafe. Look, I know this may sound crazy because you should be in Florida, but I'd swear I saw you at the hospital when I was discharged, and Alice says she saw you near my house yesterday." He paused a beat. "Are you here in Virginia? I don't know what's going on, but I need to know that I'm not crazy. Call me."

He exhaled and put the phone into the back pocket of his jeans just as Alice came through the front door with a shopping bag and headed straight for the kitchen, bypassing Rafe in the living room.

" 'Mornin'."

"Hey, good morning." He followed her into the kitchen and watched her unpack the shopping bag. "Alice, we couldn't possibly need more food in here."

Her brows shot up and then drew together. "What would you know? Fast as I fix it, it's gone." She threw her hands helplessly up in the air.

Rafe came over, wrapped her in a bear hug and kissed her cheek. "That's 'cause you put some of that black-girl magic in every pot."

She swatted him away. "Oh, go on. How's that leg?" She put clear plastic bags of fresh vegetables in the refrigerator bin.

"Good." He instinctively rubbed the area. "Stronger."

"You eat yet? Hungry?"

"I'm good. Don't worry about me."

"Been worryin' about you since forever." She waved her hand in dismissal. "I'll fix something. Then get to the laundry."

"Why do you ask if you're gonna do what you want anyway?" He took a grape from the bowl and popped it in his mouth.

"To make you think you're in charge!" she said.

Rafe chuckled and wagged a finger at her. "Right."

"You make that call?" she asked. She took a tray of eggs and put them on the table.

"Yeah . . . I did."

Alice stopped puttering and stared at him. "And?"

"No answer. I left a message."

"Humph. That thing worried me all night long." She shook her head and then began cracking eggs in a bowl.

"Anyway, we'll see if she calls back. I'm going to the gym. Haven't been able to work out in more than a month. Making me crazy."

"Maybe you shouldn't fall out of planes, and you wouldn't have that problem."

"Love you, too," he called out as he headed down to the basement.

"Don't overdo it!"

"Yes, ma'am. But I gotta get in shape. Getting married in two months!"

Avery walked past several of her seated colleagues to the front of the small conference room, opened her laptop and turned on the big screen. After several link connections her computer was paired to the big screen.

"Good morning, everyone."

The hum of "good morning" rounded the rectangular table. There were a dozen agents present from the joint task force that had been hand-selected by Avery, the director of the FBI and Homeland Security. As she took a brief look around the table she was pleased at the diversity — a good mix of not only cultures and gender, but expertise.

"As you all know for several months Homeland Security has been receiving chatter emanating from these areas." She pointed to spots on the map to areas of Turkey. "We have reason to believe that some kind of plan is in the works. Our intel suggests that it will be a cyberattack, much like what happened to the credit-reporting agencies, Wells Fargo and the pharmaceutical companies last year, only bigger, more widespread and potentially crippling. Mike, would you bring everyone up to speed with what we know so far."

Avery took a seat and all eyes turned toward Mike. As she listened to his detailed explanation and precise intel she was once again reassured that she'd made the right decision in bringing him on board. They may have had their problems over the years, but she could never deny that Mike was one helluv an agent and investigator. He'd actually turned down the promotion that would have been hers in order to join this team. To her that spoke volumes about his character and dedication.

"In your folders I've prepared a list of all the possible targets that we anticipate being hit."

Everyone opened the red folders and began to scan the list.

"Wall Street, the stock market?" one of the agents said.

"Any attack on Wall Street would create worldwide panic and instability," Mike responded. "*And* we have elections coming up. We know what happened last time. It's inevitable that another attempt will be made, and we have it on good information that it will be. We have teams fanned out across the country, evaluating the voting machines and registration sites."

"Thanks, Mike," Avery said. "In the coming days you'll begin receiving your assignment and your partner. I need everyone to stay on task. As we know there is no item that is too small or insignificant. Don't ignore anything, no matter the source, even if its 1600. Understood?"

"Yes, ma'am," they chorused.

"Thank you, everyone."

The team dispersed, but Mike hung back.

"I haven't really had a chance to tell you thanks."

Avery glanced up and tucked her laptop and folders under her arm. "For what?" She pressed a button and turned off the big screen.

"For asking me to be part of this team."

"Nothing to thank me for, Mike. You're a damned good agent."

"That I know," he joked and got her to smile. "I also know that I've been a real prick, but whatever I threw at you, you let it go, rose above it. A page right out of Michelle Obama's playbook," he added with admiration.

Avery smiled slightly. "Mike, after it's all said and done, the bottom line is it's about the work, what we're charged to do. It's about protecting the public, keeping us safe and stopping anyone or anything that threatens our way of life. We took an oath. That's what I think about."

Mike nodded with understanding.

They walked together to the door.

"How are the wedding plans coming?"

"Full steam ahead now that Rafe is fully recovered."

"Lucky man."

"That he is," she said with a smile and walked with an extra bounce to her step back to her office.

When she got off work she was thrilled to find Rafe waiting for her in the lobby.

She beamed with delight. "What are you doing here?" She gave him a quick kiss and then looked him up and down. "Suit *and* tie?"

"We haven't been out on a date in much too long. Figured tonight was the night. I made reservations."

"Reservations! Rafe, look at me. Dark blue pantsuit, white blouse. I reek 'government,' " she joked.

Rafe put his arm around her shoulder. "You could wear a sack and still be beautiful to me. Preferably a short one to show off those fabulous legs that I love wrapped around my back," he said into her ear.

A shiver scurried up her spine. She nudged him in the side. "You always know how to charm a girl. So, where are we going?"

He held the glass-and-chrome door open for her. "The Lafayette."

"How in the world did you get reservations? It's usually weeks."

"I wish I could take all the credit. I told my father I wanted to take my girl out — someplace special. He put in a call."

Avery giggled. "Pays to have people in high places."

CHAPTER 30

The Lafayette was located inside the Hay Adams hotel on 16th Street Northwest, a stone's throw away from the White House. Although renowned for its exquisite cuisine, there were few restaurants that could compare to The Lafayette's décor and superior service.

"At least I have on heels," Avery murmured as they approached the maître d's podium.

"Good evening. Welcome to The Lafayette. Reservations?"

"Yes. Lawson."

"Oh, yes. Of course. Your table is ready. Let us take your coats." He signaled one of the staff.

Rafe helped Avery out of her white trench coat and handed it over.

A waitress appeared. The maître d' murmured something to her.

She turned to Rafe and Avery. "I'll show

you to your table. Please follow me."

They were shown to a semi-private dining area with an incredible view of the DC skyline, which was already lighting up for the approaching evening. The iconic outline of the White House stood out against the twilight.

Rafe helped Avery into her seat. "Fan-cy," she murmured and bit back a cheesy grin.

"Only the best for my woman." He kissed her cheek and then took his seat.

They were seated near the pianist, who teased the keys with soft music for a perfect backdrop.

The waitress appeared and poured sparkling water into crystal goblets that seemed to shimmer like diamonds when hit by the soft light from the chandeliers. She placed a menu in front of each of them and recited the specials for the evening. "I would recommend for an appetizer the lobster-and-butternut-squash soup and for your entrees perhaps the pan-seared halibut fillet sautéed with maitake mushrooms, white wine, togarashi spice and a side of wild rice pilaf. Or if you prefer a meat dish I would recommend our Shenandoah Valley rack of lamb. It is lamb croquettes, with ratatouille, lamb jus seasoned with Georgian spice."

"Everything sounds delicious," Rafe said.

"Can I get your drink orders while you decide?"

Rafe deferred to Avery.

"Apple martini."

"Bourbon."

The waitress gave a short nod and hurried off.

Avery folded her hands on the white-linen-topped table and admired the inlaid walls that framed the portraits and landscapes of Renoir, van Gogh, Basquiat and others whom she couldn't name.

"So, tell me, what prompted date-night?"

"Just felt like we were falling into a routine and a change in atmosphere was in order."

The waitress returned with their drinks and they placed their orders for the house specials. Rafe opted for the lamb and Avery took the halibut.

They raised their glasses and toasted to their happiness.

"Did you work on any of your music today? I'm eager to hear it."

"Coming along. Didn't get as much done as I wanted to. Was actually listening to some stuff that Quinten sent over."

She tilted her head to the side in question. "And . . ."

"Just got me thinking about how much I miss playing on stage."

She reached across the table and covered his hand. "Then you have to play. You're back on your feet. Nothing is stopping you."

"Actually, me and Q have talked about playing together again at the upcoming jazz festivals — the big ones, Monterey, New Orleans, New Port, Montreal, and there's also Tuscan. That one's pretty new but getting a lot of buzz."

The appetizer arrived.

"Oh, God, this smells good," Avery said. She snapped open her napkin. "Then you have to go. Simple as that." She took a spoonful of soup and her eyes closed in rapture.

"Starting to look into it. We'll finalize everything after the wedding." He winked.

Avery pushed out a sigh. "Another month. I have to admit. I know I gave you a hard time about your sisters taking over the wedding, but the truth is I don't know what I would have done without them. I mean Dominique is a one-woman machine," she said and laughed.

"That she is."

"I mean she's handled everything from finding the perfect invitations, color scheme, the flowers, linens, selecting the menu, locating the designer down here to design my gown." She shook her head in amazement.

"No one could be happier than me that it all worked out," he chuckled.

Avery laughed along with him.

The waitress returned with their entrees and between bites of the mouth-watering food they talked about the wedding and their planned trip to Bali for their honeymoon, and Rafe broached the topic of house hunting.

"I'm thinking that your place is fine for the time being. It's close to your office. But I'd really like something that's *ours.*"

She put her fork down and leaned in. "Are you sure you're okay with moving down here to DC? I know how much you love New Orleans."

"When I'm with you, cher, anyplace is home. I have everything worked out at the foundation, the housing projects are moving along. I can play music anywhere. It's all good. Besides, I'm a phone call, Skype or a plane ride away."

"My place doesn't have an in-home studio or gym *or* Alice."

"While you're at the office doing spy stuff, I can work out or record at my place. I'm pretty sure Alice would be happy to help out."

She sighed. "Sounds like a plan."

He lifted his head a bit and looked at her from beneath lush dark lashes. "My plans don't end there."

"Meaning?"

"I have a little surprise for you."

Her eyes lit up. "What? Tell me."

"If I told you, it wouldn't be a surprise. After dessert. Promise."

She huffed. "Fine."

After a dessert of strawberry soufflé, Rafe paid the bill and collected Avery's coat. When they got to the exit, Rafe asked Avery to wait while he went to the car, which she thought was crazy, since they were leaving.

He returned shortly with his trusty go-bag and a black garment bag.

"What is going on?"

"Date night isn't over yet, darlin'."

He guided her past the restaurant through the lobby of the Hay Adams hotel to the check-in desk.

"Rafe . . ."

He held her hand. "Reservation for Lawson."

"One moment, sir." The clerk checked the computer and glanced up with a smile. "I see you'll be with us for one night, Mr. Lawson, in the penthouse suite."

"Yes." He turned to Avery and winked.

"How many keys will you need?"

"Two."

"Any luggage?"

"No. Just us." He grinned and pulled Avery close.

"The bellman will take you up to your room. Enjoy your stay."

"Thanks."

A red-vested young man appeared as if by magic, took Rafe's bags and took them up to the penthouse floor and opened the door for them.

"There is a full bar and separate seating and dining area." He opened double doors. "Master bedroom with an en suite bath. There is a second bathroom down this short hallway. And there is seating on the balcony, as well." He turned to Rafe. "Anything you need, someone at the front desk will assist you."

"Thank you." He reached in his pocket, took out his wallet and handed the young man a sizeable tip.

"Thank you, Mr. Lawson. Mrs. Lawson. Enjoy your stay."

The instant the door closed behind him, Rafe swept Avery into his arms. "Mrs. Lawson. Love the sound of that."

"Me, too," she said softly. "You had this all planned out. You're pretty good at keeping secrets."

Inwardly he twinged with guilt. Yeah, he was getting good at secret-keeping. "Only when necessary."

"What's in the bag?"

"I took the liberty of selecting your outfit for tomorrow." He laid the garment bag on the bed and unzipped it. "Voilà."

Avery burst into laughter. "Dark suit, white blouse."

Rafe shrugged. "Aw, that's nothing. The real goodies are in my go-bag."

"I can only imagine." She rubbed up against him.

"And I ordered some champagne."

"Of course you did," she said, and kissed him like she'd been wanting to kiss him all evening.

It was clear that Rafe was fully recovered in every respect. There wasn't an inch of her body that he'd left untouched. Her blood still simmered, her skin still tingled. Would it always be like this between them? Would she always need him like the air she breathed? It was a scary thought for the girl who only needed her wits and her gun.

She eased out of bed, careful not to wake him, and tiptoed to the sitting area. In a few hours she'd have to be up and ready for work but for some reason she was restless, unsettled in a way that she couldn't quite get her head around. They'd had an amazing evening. Not one wrong note. They'd talked and laughed and made real plans. There was no reason not to be curled up next to her man, deep in the throes of sleep. Instead she sat in the dark — looking as she always did for the boogeyman.

A buzzing noise coming from the end table drew her attention. The light from the cell phone lit up the darkness. She reached for the phone and her breath caught. The phone continued to vibrate until she crossed the invisible line and answered Rafe's phone.

"Janae . . . please don't hang up." She heard the quick intake of breath. "This is Avery."

"I shouldn't have called."

"But you did. I need you to tell me why." When she didn't get an answer, she continued. "I know that he came to see you. Rafe told me everything. I can't even imagine what you've been through." She waited a beat. "It was you at the hospital when he was discharged wasn't it?"

"Yes. But you have to believe me, I didn't want to cause any problems. I needed to see for myself that he was okay."

Avery heard the pain in her voice and a part of her heart went out to the woman who'd loved him first.

"I came to his house the other day."

"What?"

"I didn't see him. No one answered the door. I don't know what I was thinking other than I was going back to my life in Florida, and it might be the last time I'd ever see him. I think Alice may have recognized me as I was driving away. I'm not sure."

Her head was spinning.

"I'm . . . actually returning Rafe's call. After I came by the house he called me wanting to know if it was me at the hospital and his house, and what was I doing in DC. I didn't get his message until I landed in Florida." She paused a moment. "There was a part of me that believed I could never let him go. But when I saw him with you, the way he looked at you, the way you looked at him, I knew it was time. I came by the house to tell him that and see him for the last time. He's happy and in love with you, and all he and I ever wanted for each other was our happiness. He's an incredible man and when he's all in, he's all in. Take care of him. He deserves it more than anyone I've ever known."

"I will."

"Avery, you okay? What are you doing up?" He rubbed sleep from his eyes as he stood in the arch of the doorway, silhouetted by the moonlight.

Avery drew in a breath and slowly stood. She crossed the room and handed him the phone. "Someone needs to speak with you. It's okay." She kissed his cheek and returned to the bedroom. This time she slept through the night.

EPILOGUE

The first weekend in June arrived in spectacular fashion. The cloudless sky was coupled with a hint of a warm breeze, which was just enough to lift a curl, stir the blooms that lined the walkway leading into the church or ruffle the tulle skirts of the bridesmaids. After months of planning, near losses, breakups and makeups, the day they'd dreamed about had arrived.

The white velvet runner led from the door of the church to be met on either side of the altar with five-foot urns overflowing with Sprengeri ferns, and bridal veil, mixed with Queen Anne's lace and light pink and lilac roses. The pillars and pews sprouted feather-light ferns and baby's breath, giving the entire space a fairy-tale feel. Melanie Harte, long-time family friend, matchmaker extraordinaire and premier party planner, had worked with Dominique to decorate the church and plan out the reception, which was to take place later at the Lawson mansion.

There was no getting away from the press, but Avery no longer cared as she exited the stretch limo — a vision in white, diamonds and pearls — and was hustled into the church by her bridesmaids, to shouts of "turn this way," clicks of reporters' cameras and what would certainly be cell-phone video.

They entered the church vestibule and were directed by an attendant to the ladies-in-waiting room.

"Perfect," Dominique announced the instant they opened the door.

Two overstuffed couches, comfy side chairs, a portable rack for hanging clothing, a food cart with light snacks and bottles of ice water and ceramic white bowls of floating calla lilies waited for them, and a full bathroom finished off the area.

Avery's gown rustled softly as she entered and looked around. Her throat tightened. She turned to Dominique, who was busy fussing with the flowers. She placed her hand on Dominique's shoulder.

Dominique turned, wide-eyed. "Everything okay?" The beaded bodice of her cocktail dress twinkled under the lights.

"Dom," she turned toward her sisters-in-law to be, "Lee Ann, Desi, I really . . . I can't thank you all enough. I know I was being bitchy and difficult in the beginning, but none of this," she looked around and waved her hand, "would have happened without you." She put her arm around Kerry. "While Kerry was keeping my head screwed on straight and making sure that I didn't run away from the most wonderful man in the world, ya'll were here making all this happen." She took a breath and blinked hard to stem a flow of tears. "Thank you."

"You're family," Dominique said. "And Rafe's our big brother. He loves you and we love you, too."

"And don't even start crying and messing up your makeup," Desiree said, surprisingly fit only two months after having her twins.

"Besides," Lee Ann added, "we were just happy to get that man settled down with someone who could tame that wild side. Now you can deal with him!"

The sisters laughed in agreement.

Avery sniffed and laughed along with them. She was ready and one thing she knew for sure was that her new sisters would have her back.

"Make sure that you eat a little something," Lee Ann advised. "So you don't get light-headed."

"I will. Promise." She turned and was awestruck at her reflection in the full-length mirror.

Kerry came up behind her and placed her hands on Avery's shoulders. "Ready?" She adjusted Avery's tiara.

"Girl, I'm more than ready to marry my man."

"You and me both!"

There was a light knock on the room door.

"Come in," Avery called out. She turned around on the stool. Her father stepped in. "Dad."

"Look at my baby." He smiled in admiration.

"I'll leave you two alone," Kerry whispered and then eased out with Rafe's sisters.

Horace Richards stepped fully into the room. "You look beautiful. Just like your mother."

Avery drew in a deep breath. "I wish she was here."

"She's watching over you, sweetheart." He pulled up a chair and sat. "I know I haven't been the best father —"

"Dad, you don't —"

"No. You need to hear this. I don't think I ever got over losing your mother. We had our troubles, but I loved her. I guess I believed that if I allowed myself to love you like I should have, I'd lose you, too. So I kept my distance, closed off my heart. I was hard on you. But I still only wanted the best for you. I wanted you to be tough, independent so that you could never be hurt." He paused. "And I'm sorry. So very sorry. I love you, sweetheart, and you now have someone to love and care for you. The way it should be."

"Oh, Daddy." She leaned into his arms and pressed her cheek to his. This was what she'd wanted all her life. To hear him say those words, and she finally understood with vivid clarity that they were more alike than different. She'd fought off love and being loved the same way her father did.

Kerry poked her head back in the door. "They're getting ready to play your song."

Avery straightened and beamed at her dad. "You ready to give me away."

Horace stood. "Never. But I know you'll be in good hands."

The bridal party was led in by Lee Ann and Justin, followed by Desiree and Spence, and Dominique and Trevor. Then the maid of honor, Kerry, and best man, Quinten, walked in to Luther Vandross's "Here and Now." Once in their places, the attendants opened the doors to the sanctuary. The congregation rose to their feet as Rafe and Avery's wedding song, "When I'm With You," began to play.

When Rafe set eyes on Avery, walking down the aisle on the arm of her father, it felt like a dream. He'd never seen her look more surreal, more magnificently beautiful as she appeared to float along the white runner that led to the altar.

The fitted gown embossed with hundreds of hand-sewn pearls and splashes of diamonds hugged her body, save for the dangerous right-side split that stopped mid-thigh. The tiara crown sparkled beneath the lights, but nothing was brighter than the smile she held for her husband to be.

When Avery stood to face Rafe at the altar, she couldn't tear her eyes away from him. This was it, their moment. They'd been through hell and back. They'd survived.

"Dearly beloved . . ."

Branford and Jacqueline sat in a place of honor as she tried and failed to stem the tears that rolled down her cheeks. Branford turned to his sister, took her hand and held it.

"Who gives this woman to this man?"

Horace stepped forward, gazed lovingly at his daughter. "I do," he said with a catch in his throat. He kissed her cheek and stepped aside.

"Do you, Avery Aleise Richards, take Raford Beaumont Lawson as your husband . . . ?"

"I do."

"Do you, Raford Beaumont Lawson, take Avery Aleise Richards as your lawfully wedding wife . . . ?"

"The rings please."

Avery turned to Kerry and took the ring for Rafe. Quinten handed Rafe the ring.

"I understand you have something to say, Rafe," the minister said.

Rafe took Avery's hand and slid the blinding diamond on her finger. "Avery, I knew the moment I met you that you were meant for me. I just didn't know how much. You've stuck with me. Understood me, made me believe after all that had happened that I could love again. You made me want to live life again. When I'm with you, I know that anything is possible, and I can't wait to start our life together and all the possibilities. I love you, cher."

Avery could barely keep the tears from her eyes. "Rafe." She took his hand and slid on the platinum-and-diamond band. "I was scared, difficult to deal with and unsure. I thought all I needed in life was a career.

But you never gave up no matter how hard I pushed you away. You just kept on loving me. I want to spend the rest of my life loving you and basking in your love for me. We can accomplish anything together. Our love is unbreakable. When I'm with you, I know that there is a God because He gave me you."

"Now, by the powers vested in me, I pronounce you husband and wife. Please salute your bride."

Rafe took Avery in his arms and kissed her as if there was no one else in the world except them, and she melted into the embrace of her husband, knowing that today was the first day of the rest of their lives, and together she knew they were in for an adventure.

ABOUT THE AUTHOR

Donna Hill began writing novels in 1990. Since that time she has had more than forty titles published, which include full-length novels and novellas. Two of her novels and one novella were adapted for television. She has won numerous awards for her body of work. She is also the editor of five novels, two of which have been nominated for awards. She easily moves from romance to erotica, horror, comedy and women's fiction. She was the first recipient of the *RT Book Reviews* Trailblazer Award and won the *RT Book Reviews* Career Achievement Award. Donna lives in Brooklyn with her family. Visit her website at www.donnahill .com.